2021.

Love,

Kathleen

The

Monday After

Father's Day

Or

Revelations: A Parable

Illustrations by Tilly Castelli
Map by Ken Castelli
Cover Photo by Jay Fleming
Author Photo by Bennet Price
Cover Design by Zack Schmitt

Published in the United States by
Head to Wind Publishing
PO Box 74
Galena, MD 21635

HEAD⚓WIND
PUBLISHING

A Johnsontown Novella

By

Pete Fortenbaugh

Dedication

I want to dedicate this book to Mom and Dad for raising me amongst great books and stories, and for being the best parents anyone could ask for. To publisher Nancy Robson for making this book possible. And to the late, great Whid Eskridge for opening his home to me, giving me a job and being such a great friend.

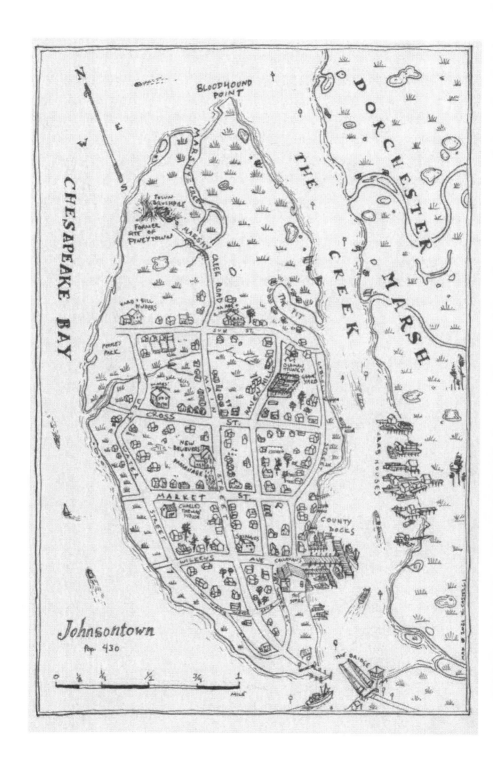

Johnsontown ca. 2019

Charles Thomas had made up his mind to find Jesus first thing that Monday morning to see if Jesus could work a miracle on that broke arm of his, and maybe if He could do a little thing like that, He might really could bring back the dead. It had been exactly a week since some of the older boys on the island had convinced Charles Thomas to test their parachute, and since then Charles Thomas had come to know that seven summer days with a busted arm were seven days lost and seven days too many. He was pretty well done sitting around in the air conditioning with a throbbing arm, watching TV and eating ice cream. He'd only had seven summers so far, and this one — now that he was eight and finally a free man to roam or bike around the island as he pleased, to swim or skiff, to fish or crab, or to play ball when the older boys let him — he'd be dernt if a broke arm meant he had to miss out on all that.

Charles Thomas got up when he heard his Mom trundle out their little lane, her grasscutter tied behind her bike, to cut yards all around the island of Johnsontown[1]. The early light was reddish and secrety inside the house. The boy didn't turn on any lights; he just slipped on his fiery red swimming trunks and a grey, knee-length Big Dog t-shirt before making his way to the kitchen. He climbed up onto the counter to make his Frosted Flakes, sneaking two extra spoonfuls from the sugar jar that his Mom would never know about.

He winced when he picked up the gallon of milk with both hands. The new, neon-orange club on his right forearm made all kinda little things awkward, and his arm inside pained him something terrible near all the time. Their black cat, Batman, leapt up on the counter, and Charles Thomas spilled a little extra milk for Batman to

---

[1] Johnsontown is a small, isolated island in Maryland's Chesapeake Bay. The island is roughly 3 miles long, 1.5 miles at its greatest width, and barely 6 feet above sea level at its highest point. Jtown (as it is affectionately known) is home to roughly 430 people, a large part of whom are tied in some way to working the water: harvesting crabs, fish and oysters from the surrounding waters of the Bay as islanders have for nearly four centuries. Due to its location, and its low, soft landmass, the island is extremely vulnerable to erosion and sea level rise, meaning that Johnsontown may become one of America's first casualties to climate change in the decades to come.

lick up. The boy liked to chitchat with the cat when no one else was around.

Batman lapped up the milk, then raised his head and grumbled in that gravely, island-accented Dark Knight voice of his: *I thank ye thare, C.T.*

"Anything fer you, Mr. Wayne," Charles Thomas replied.

Yer a good man, ye are.

"Ye ain't so bad yerself, Mr. Wayne."

Hey, do me a favor will ye and keep that 'Mr. Wayne' stuff on the down-low, Charles Thomas.

"Shoot I'm done fergot agin."

Lookee hyare: yer got ta remember we're in a battle a' Good versus Evil hyare. And you know if them Bad Guys find out certain secrets we're all screwed, glued and tattooed.

"Yer Secrets is safe with me, Batman."

And yourn with me, Charles Thomas.

Charles Thomas and the cat carried on their little habitual conversation until the cat ran off. See, Charles Thomas didn't have to worry about making noise as he ate: he and his Mom and Batman lived alone. His Father had left them, and left the island, because, as his Mom said, he'd really wanted to, and so that made him as good as dead.

From his place on the counter Charles Thomas got to studying the painting of Jesus that his Mom had hanging above the supper table. He'd always loved the picture. It felt so familiar, like someone he'd always known. Jesus had this gold ring around His head and these soft brown eyes; just like the ones that Charles Thomas saw looking back at him from the mirror (which certainly meant something). And Jesus had this look on His face like He was about to say, *You know what, Charles Thomas: if I had me a son, I'd want him to be just like you,* before giving Charles Thomas a brand new Ipad, or new outboard or something like that. And Charles Thomas knew you could trust the things He said and the things He gave.

Who or exactly what Jesus Christ was, was something Charles Thomas couldn't ever exactly say for sure. Man, spirit, living, dead, the Son of God, the Son of Man, in the clouds, on the earth, everywhere at once. Dast, it was enough to make your head swim. These were questions Charles Thomas had wondered over near as long as he could think, but when that Visitin Preacher spoke, it all suddenly seemed clear as the churchbell: Jesus lived. He was right here on Johnsontown, and He'd do anything you asked of Him. All you had to do was track Him down. It was just that simple.

That Visitin Preacher, who had come to talk to the New Believers'[2] Sunday School class the day before, had looked something like Jesus. He had long, dark hair, a big beard and soft, dark eyes. He was wearing loose, baggy, all-white clothes with no tie. He looked cool. Even the older boys admitted that. And he had him this funny voice that sounded like Colonel Sanders, or the rooster from Looney Toons. And that man had him a way with the electric guitar, and a way of singing that made him seem so dern important. But more than all that, the man had a gift with the Word. The way he explained it all, the way he moved around and drew pictures with his hands in the air above Charles Thomas and the other kids: it was like he was conducting an orchestra, or was a general motivating an army. For Charles Thomas it was like magic; he couldn't look away.

It had been a Father's Day sermon. The Visitin Preacher had started by talking to them about how Jesus

---

[2] The New Believers Church of Christ is Johnsontown's Evangelical church. The New Believers split from the island's more traditional Ephraim Price First United Methodist Church in the early '90s, causing a vicious schism that has never fully healed.

loved them like his own children, and how much the Father loved Jesus and how much Jesus loved the Father. Then he talked for a long while about finding Jesus, bringing Him into their lives and homes and living with Him. He kept telling them that Jesus was here with them, just like a member of the family. How He was all around them, right here on Johnsontown! And how it was up to them to go forth seeking Him with their hearts opened to His powers. Then that Visitin Preacher told them how it had to be now or never, because that final Day of Days was near at hand. He told it like an awesome superhero movie, just how The End would come. How the sun would turn black and the moon blood red, and how the stars would fall to earth. He said the Heavens would roll up like a paper map and every island and mountain would be removed from its place. Then he told them how on that Final Day Jesus would call up his army of angels and come riding down from the clouds on a white horse, His legs afire, and a fiery sword springing from His mouth, set to harvest the heads of sinners and non-believers. Charles Thomas loved imagining Christ like that, like a super-superhero. He loved imagining that great Final Battle, himself (castless) beside Christ, cutting up sinners and demons with a sword, and then being chosen by Jesus to climb up into the sky and take his place between his Father and his Savior.

Charles Thomas had got so lost in imagining all of that he'd only half heard the Visitin Preacher go on talking about Faith for what seemed like an eternity. But then his ears perked up again when that Visitin Preacher got to talking about miracles. About Jesus making the lame walk and the blind see, and dead old Lazarus sitting straight up from his grave. That Visitin Preacher told them of the miracles he'd seen worked with his own eyes, beneath his very hands: stutters vanished; cancer was cured; a child rose from a wheelchair; bones were healed! And then all of a sudden, the man was pointing at Charles Thomas.

"You, boy, what's yow name?"

Charles Thomas heard himself saying, "Um, well, I'm Charles Thomas Parks." He wasn't used to introducing himself to people.

The feller smiled real big, like off-island adults are liable to do, and he said, "Well Charles, how would you–"

Charles Thomas had had to cut that cool Visitin Preacher off right there.

"I ain't Charles. I'm Charles Thomas. Charles is o'er thare," he said pointing across the room towards little Charles Pinder.

The Visitin Preacher had laughed at that and said, "My humble apologies Charles *Thomas*. You got you quite a name there, boy. Two saints in one!" He'd laughed at his own joke and flipped his long hair out his eyes and then asked, "Charles Thomas, you wanna come up here for a moment?"

Next thing Charles Thomas knew, there he was beside the Visitin Preacher, up there in front of the whole Sunday School class with all them older boys and everybody else looking up at him. The Visitin Preacher asked him what had happened to his arm, and before he could say a word everybody started laughing. They all knew the whole story of the parachute test. When the crowd had calmed down Charles Thomas told that Visitin Preacher the story, and the man had laughed, too.

But then the feller got real serious and put his hands on Charles Thomas's cast and the throbbing arm inside and said, "Come on now kids, I want you to pray for Charles Thomas. I want you to pray just as hard as you can now. Pray for little Charles Thomas's arm. Pray that his arm may be healed through the miracles of Christ! Pray for Jesus to come to him and fill his life right to the brim with the Fire of the Spirit! Pray for him! Come on now, pray!"

For a long while they all sat there like that with their eyes closed – Charles Thomas peeking out at them through his pinched lids from time to time to check that they were really praying for him – and then the Visitin Preacher cleared his throat again and asked,

"How about it, Charles Thomas? Do you feel the Spirit burnin within you?"

Charles Thomas had consulted that little cave within himself that he thought of as his soul, and he'd figured he could pretty well see and feel a flame burning like one of them torches Indiana Jones might make.

"Yeah, I reckon so," he'd told the Visitin Preacher, "Sure 'nough, I reckon so."

"And how about that arm of yours? It feeling any better?"

His arm throbbed on inside the cast, but it was also tingling slightly there beneath the Visitin Preacher's big, hairy hands. It didn't quite feel fixed, but Charles Thomas didn't want to let the feller down, so he'd said, "Yeuh, I 'magine it feels a hair better. I thank ye, Mr. Visitin Preacher, sir."

The man flicked his hair and laughed again.

"And Charles Thomas, you know what you got to do now, don't you?"

Charles Thomas had made no gesture, nor sound. The truth was he hadn't had the slightest clue exactly what he had to do now. But he did know one thing: he sure weretn't gonna let the whole world know what he didn't know! And so he kept his face focused in a sort of grimace and gave a little nod. The Visitin Preacher smiled again.

"Charles Thomas you've got to get out there after our Lord Jesus Christ. You've got to find His love and His light. You've got to open your heart, open it wide, and take in His words and His teachings. Take it to heart! For Jesus, He's been waiting here, here on this very island, right beside you all your life and more! He's just waiting for you to go to Him so He can work His miracles for you! Remember, Charles Thomas, what Jesus told His disciples in Matthew seven, verse seven, He said, 'Ask and it will be given to you; seek and you will find; knock and the door will be opened to you. For everyone that asks receives; the one who seeks finds; and for the one who knocks...? That door will be opened!'"

"That's right 'n tight, sure 'nough it is," Charles Thomas said, nodding his head along just like older church folk did. And with that, finally, the Visitin Preacher patted his shoulder and gave him a little push back to his seat.

"Thank you, Charles Thomas. Now make haste, and go forth seeking the miracles and salvation of Our Lord and Savior Jesus Christ, Amen."

Charles Thomas had come out of church that evening with his body and soul aflame. He'd felt he could lift a house, broke arm and all. Miracles were possible and Christ was at hand, for Charles Thomas knew the Spirit had entered him; when he closed his eyes and imagined just right he could see its torch burning within him. He'd tried at supper to explain what he'd seen and heard to his Mom, his Uncle Furry, his Aunt Sally and the others gathered around the table. They all seemed pleased as could be, and had praised the Visitin Preacher some. But at the same time, Charles Thomas felt like he couldn't quite communicate the power that he'd felt, and as conversation moved on he'd watched his flame flicker and shrink before their smiles and approval, as if by voicing the feeling it had become less real. They'd eaten a big supper (fried perch, chicken and dumplings, and crab cobbler) and by the time supper was over and everyone had left, Charles Thomas was feeling all weighted down as if a stone were around his middle.

Just before bed, Charles Thomas had crawled out his bedroom window onto his little slice of kitchen roof to watch for falling stars as he sometimes did. He lay on his back, the weight pressing down and the cold gritty shingles itching his skin. His arm was throbbing in its cast irregardless of everyone's prayers. The moon was nearly full, and only the brightest stars made sharp holes in the moon's creamy light. He closed his eyes and focused, and he was flooded with happiness, for he found if he concentrated hard enough he could see and feel the flame that the Visitin Preacher had lit was burning on, bright and piercing as the distant stars. He opened his eyes and stared at the sky, thinking about things. Finally, a falling star appeared, and Charles Thomas shut his eyes again and dove into a prayer: *Please Lord, will ye fix my arm up so it don't hurt so bad all the time, and help me to find Jesus so that he might work these miracles. And maybe also, if you could, bring my Father back and make everybody happier again, Amen.*

Soon as Charles Thomas finished his prayer he heard a rumbling in his head from what he liked to call his Prayer Voice, a sort of friend that spoke to him in a basey voice and guided him from time to time. (And Charles Thomas's Prayer Voice was not some stupid imaginary friend like little kids might have; no, his Prayer Voice was as real and solid and comforting as footsteps on a wood floor above your head.) That Voice said to him, *Don't you worry, you'll find Jesus awright, Charles Thomas, and He'll fix ye up good as gets*, and Charles Thomas had a nice chat with his Prayer Voice that left him feeling pretty good.

When he'd finished praying, Charles Thomas opened his eyes and looked up at the numberless stars burning in the Heavens. He lay there in half-sleep, imagining all of that rolling up like a paper map. He imagined all those stars falling to the Earth as that great Final Battle raged. Imagined Christ and his army of angels hurling mountains at the sinners and the devils, while all the Good Guys fought together. Himself swinging a fiery sword – like a light saber only cooler – cutting dragons and awful demons to pieces. And then, in The End, Jesus would come and choose him. He'd reach His hand down and carry Charles Thomas up into the sky to take his place beside his Father and his Savior so they could live happily ever after in the light of all eternity.

But then his Prayer Voice brought up that old nagging question: *Who's to say when that final Day of Days is gonna come Charles Thomas? Could be next year, or the year after that, or even the year after that!*

But the Visitin Preacher had changed all that. He didn't have to wait – for Christ was here on the island, here and now, and He'd do anything you asked of Him if you could just track Him down. Charles Thomas's eyes were heavy with all that thinking. He'd let them close, and dreamed in the light of this new flame, dreaming of the miracles Jesus would work for him. The light grew strong and shone like a searchlight through his shadowy dreams until the summer night's chill woke him and he'd climbed woodenly through the window to bed. There, in the safe warmth of bed, he'd promised himself that first thing in the morning he'd get to finding Jesus, to see what miracles Jesus might could work on that busted arm of his. And maybe if He could do a little thing like that, He might really could bring back the dead.

By the time Charles Thomas finished his breakfast the morning light had changed from soft red to a hard white. He could feel the heat pressing through the windowpane. It was sure gonna be hot. He heard his Prayer Voice flood his head with a strong commandment: *Gowan boy, get on out thare. You find Jesus, and dern if yer problems won't be fixed up just right.*

Without another thought, the boy hopped down to the floor and headed out the door, leaving everything behind on the counter and his teeth un-brushed.

The sun was an hour above the endless wilderness of marshes to the east of the island. It was already lashing the world with a close, breathless heat. Tide was up in the ditches across Johnsontown, and so Charles Thomas, barefoot as always, walked northward through the calf-deep water that filled the ditches of West Water St. along the island's Bayside. The dark water was warm as bathwater, and the submerged mud felt good between his toes. Grasscutters and locusts hummed all around the island. Beyond the island's shores the Bay was slick cam[3], motionless and glaring like a pool of molten metal. A good many of the white, steep-roofed houses on lower ground had water ringing their raised cinderblock foundations.

The first person the boy saw that morning was an old man called Ham slowly pumping his bike southward down West Water. Ham had lived on the island all of his ninety years, except his time in the Army during the Korean War. He called out as he worked his bike past:

"Full moon ain't got tide up none is she[4], Charles Thomas?"

---

[3] 'Slick cam': A glassy calm to the water.
[4] The people of Johnsontown speak a unique dialect, which linguists trace back to a mix between their Southern English and West African ancestors, who arrived on the island in the mid 1600's. It is incredibly rich and distinctive, with over 400 unique words and phrases not found elsewhere. Notice here the tendency to 'speak backwards' – using the

"'Magine not," the boy replied taking an appraising look at the water flooding up over his island. The old man laughed, and the creak of his rusty bike faded off down the street.

Charles Thomas followed a group of minnows dancing in the ditch. He liked to pretend that he was a giant and they were an invading army swarming his island. He kicked at a bunch that came too close. In their haste to

negative to emphasize a statement, without even a hint of irony or sarcasm.

escape, a few of the foot soldiers leapt out of the water and landed in the grass along the ditch. Charles Thomas watched their trapped, silver bodies flicking in the sun.

One cried, *Help us, Charles Thomas! We'll do anything! Please!*

Locusts thrummed in a tree close by. Charles Thomas lifted one muddy foot from the water and positioned his big toe over the wriggling, translucent body of one trapped minnow.

No, Charles Thomas! It cried. *We thought you was one a' the Good Guys!*

That's whare yer wrong, he said to it in his head, lips moving just a bit, *I am a Good Guy. It's you that works fer Evil. You and all yer water!*

Just then Charles Thomas heard the rumble of a pushmower towed behind a bike and lowered his foot back down into the water leaving the stranded fish to its fate. He looked up to see his Mom approaching.

She pedaled her bike with a weedwhacker over her shoulder and her pushmower tied behind. She had on a man's button-up shirt, a dirty hat, and loose, grass-spattered khakis. A milk jug of gas swung from a lanyard around her neck. As she neared, she hollered into the empty street:

"Bees-n-mice[5], I know if I'm tolt ye once I tolt ye a dozen times: I don't want you out-n-bout with that busted arm yer got."

"I ain't doin nothin," Charles Thomas grumbled back.

She stopped her bike and planted her tattered and stained tennis shoes on the warming asphalt.

"Ain't doin nothin!? Good Lord knows what all that can mean!"

He ignored her assault and slapped with his good hand at a blood-filled skeeter[6] that just then bit him in the soft spot behind his knee. He felt her eyes searching him like she knew he had a secret.

"I'ma wear out yer behind if you get that cast a yers wet and we're got ta buy ye a new one."

"Don't I know it," he said back. He kicked his muddy foot out at another squadron of minnows that dared to come close.

"Lord, ye ain't no trouble," she said, chuckling a bit despite herself.

---

[5] 'Bees-n-mice': An island substitute for 'Jesus Christ'. There are dozens of these unique euphemisms for curse words in the island dialect.

[6] 'Skeeter': Mosquitoes are outrageously prolific on Johnsontown due to the fact that more than half the island is marsh and standing water.

Charles Thomas went on ignoring her to the best of his abilities, until she asked, "So what ye fixin to do with yer day?"

"Nothin."

He knew well enough that you didn't go around telling people – worst of all your Mom – that you were looking for Jesus to fix your arm and bring back your Father. It was one of those things that if you talked about it, you ruined it.

"Me, I'm got [7] two more yards to cut, then I'm got ta work lunch at Skipjacks[8]. But I'ma set sumptin out on the counter for yer lunch."

"I'll be fine."

He heard her sucking in on her lips. Then he heard her change her tone: "Just be careful will ye, Sweetpea? Last thing I want is fer that arm a yer's to get no worse, and fer us to have more doctor's bills I cain't afford."

"I'm tolt ye I'll be fine. Lord, just let me be!"

---

[7] 'I'm got': This is a distinctive grammatical shift on the island. Instead of using the Present Perfect – 'I've got '– islanders tend to use a modification of the Present Continuous – 'I'm got'. Instead of 'I've been to Cambridge before' an islander would say, 'I'm been to Cambridge afore'. Instead of 'We have been' or 'You have been' it would be 'We're been' or 'Yer been.'

[8] 'Skipjacks': The only restaurant on the island.

"Awright, awright. Don't get all worked up now." She put her feet on the pedals and started trundling off down the street. "I see ye fer supper once I'm done at the restaurant. Round three-thirty or four. Supper's no later'an five."

"I see ye," Charles Thomas replied just as cold as he could.

He knew she'd want the last word. She was halfway down the block when she called that thing she often said for whole empty street to hear: "Sharper'an a snake's tooth havin ye a thankless child."

She's just a quarrelsome werman, Charles Thomas heard his Prayer Voice saying in his head.

"Terrible quarrelsome," Charles Thomas grumbled to the empty street.

She's quarrelsome, but she's as good a woman as the Lord ever made.

"If she weretn't so quarrelsome I'd still have me a Father!"

And then he had her in his head, clear as if she was still standing right beside him picking up the argument: *You know ye don't remember all that. You weretn't nare a toddler.*

Nobody wanted him to remember his Father just because Charles Thomas was only three when his Father left for good. But he remembered plenty alright! Charles Thomas remembered his Mom screaming and crying and carrying on all the time – especially late at night when she thought he was asleep. And then his Father would be gone for days at a time. Charles Thomas could remember, even then, feeling every time like he might be gone for good, and that it was all his Mom's fault. He knew the score all right. She told him he couldn't remember 'cause she ain't want him to, but he remembered plenty. He remembered clear as yesterday.

There was one day not long before his Father left for good when his Mom had been quarreling terrible. His Father had said 'nough was enough, and he took Charles Thomas out to some crabhouse in The Creek[9]. He remembered all the men laughing and smoking and holding him on their knees til they forgot he was there. He

---

[9] 'The Creek': James Creek is the harbor for Johnsontown watermen. The Creek divides Jtown from the hundreds of thousands of acres of marsh that make up the southern Dorchester County mainland. The aforementioned 'crabhouses' are small, wooden structures built on stilts along The Creek. Many watermen use them as sort of tool sheds, or slips for their boats, offices, or simply getaways from the family. However, the primary purpose of the crabhouse is for shedding peelers (see subsequent footnote).

remembered the running water in the peeler floats[10] and the reflections the light off the water made on the plywood roof. He remembered the smell of softies in wet newspaper, and a patchy black cat crunching up a dead peeler at eye level with him. But mostly he remembered the men that night: all red faces, cigarettes and tattoos, a smell that burned your eyes like rubbing alcohol, and huge laughs that came with shoves and slaps on the back.

[10] 'Peeler floats' are shallow, plywood-boxed pools used for 'shedding peelers' or molting crabs. Bay water is pumped through these boxes, and in a delicate, round-the-clock process of unique animal husbandry, these molting crabs are painstakingly cared for until they lose their outer shell and become 'softies' or soft crabs, which are then sold at 4 to 5 times the price of hard-shell crabs. Over 60% of America's soft crabs come from a few such places in the Chesapeake and are cultivated in such a way.

Long after dark his Father fell asleep in an armchair with rusty springs sticking out.

Charles Thomas had crawled up in his lap and stared into his face for a long time, like he'd known it was something precious fading away. He remembered being three and staring at that face. He remembered that it was hairy and red, but now for the life of him he couldn't picture exactly how that face looked, and in the end it always got mixed all up with his Uncle Furry's face, or the familiar painting above the supper table, or a whole bunch of other faces. And that meant that his Mom was right – he couldn't remember proper – and that made Charles Thomas madder than anything.

Nare a soul on the island had heard word-one from Charles Thomas's Father in close to five years. Not his grandparents, nor Uncle Furry, nor his Mom, nor anybody else. That meant he had to be dead, didn't it? Or else why wouldn't he want to call, or send a text, or a pigeon with a message, or something – anything! – just to find out how Charles Thomas was doing, at the very least. Sometimes Charles Thomas imagined how his Father had died being brave and suffering like a martyr, like Jesus, or Obi-Wan Kenobi or some saint. Fighting Bad Guys or dragons, shot full of arrows or fed to lions. Maybe even crucified.

Sometimes too, Charles Thomas imagined him kidnapped – captured or exiled to some island in the middle of the ocean like he's learned in Sunday School had happened to St. John. Maybe there was so much maximum security, or he was so far away, that he couldn't call, nor send a message or whatever. But that thought always made Charles Thomas feel cheated, because of course if his Father really cared, he'd of found *some* way to just let Charles Thomas know he was still thinking about him. Wouldn't he?

So in the end Charles Thomas always went back to imagining his Father's heroic death like all the great saints and martyrs: like St. Sebastian or St. Peter, or Obi-Wan or Gandalf, then imagining his Father climbing up to Heaven to take his all-seeing throne beside Christ Almighty. But for some reason, all of a sudden, death seemed so awful and final it made Charles Thomas's throat feel tight; his arm pulsed in waves like the fire siren, and his eyes smarted like he was about to cry in the middle of the street.

His Prayer Voice rumbled in just in time: *Come on now C.T. Real men don't cry!*

So the boy bit his lip to stop himself and instead tried to focus on opening his heart for Jesus. He imagined how it would be opening his heart – peeling back his chest like a sardine can, slicing his still beating heart in half. He lingered on the image for a while, feeling his flame swell. Then he conjured up the painting of Jesus over the supper table. He knew there was no one on the island that walked around in a bed sheet, or had a glowing circle around his head – but it was a painting after all, and everybody knew paintings weren't real. Charles Thomas wished he could get his hands on a photo of Jesus, and he wracked his brain on where he might have seen one. Whoever Jesus was, Charles Thomas knew he had long hair and a beard and had to be the nicest and funniest and bestest man on the island.

The first person that came to mind right away was his Uncle Furry. Furry had been Charles Thomas's Father's older brother. Now he was just Charles Thomas's Uncle. Furry led the men's prayer group at New Believers, and he could quote the Bible a hundred different ways. He also had these two blurry crosses tattooed atop of his forearms, and he always had time for Charles Thomas, and would ride him around the island on his motorcycle, making jokes and talking to everybody, especially pretty women. And Furry did great magic tricks, and that was close to miracles. The problem was Furry never got in off the water until 11 a.m. at the earliest, so if Charles Thomas was trying to find Jesus he'd have to start with other possibilities.

The other idea Charles Thomas had as he made his way north up West Water Street was of Rooster Reed. Rooster had a massive beard and long curly hair like the painting. His hair was mostly grey, but Jesus might be old by now. And Rooster was a carpenter, too! He would tie your shoe, or ride you around the island in the back of his truck, and at Christmas time Rooster always dressed up as Santy Claus and handed out the presents at the firehouse. That being said, even babies knew that Rooster ran the island poker table. And that the winter before Rooster had crashed his truck through the First Methodist fence when he was three sheets to the wind. And those were both things Charles Thomas knew to be the same as flirting with the Devil. But Charles Thomas remembered that the Devil came and talked to Jesus a couple times, so…maybe the Devil was still trying to tempt Jesus? The good thing was Rooster always had time to talk, and he was funnier than Homer Simpson. And, most importantly, Charles Thomas knew where Rooster would be – for the last four months Rooster had been working on the island mailman Bill Pinder's house on Sun Street, just a block and a half away.

Bill and Barb Pinder's house was at the corner of West Water and Sun Street, right next to People's Park. There were a handful of younger kids playing on the jungle gym and the swings in the park – their moms all standing by, chatting and watching. Charles Thomas ignored them; being eight he was too old these days for swings and jungle gyms. As he'd expected, Rooster's rusted-out truck was parked in the street, and he spotted Miss Barb in her front yard weeding her garden. Charles Thomas let himself in Miss Barb's front gate and started his way nimbly up her oyster shell path.

"Mornin, Miss Barb."

"Mornin thare, Mr. Charles Thomas. The Good Lord woked up smilin today, ain't He," she said, nodding to the cloudless sky. Miss Barb was a very large, red-faced woman who sent every island child a card and a cookie for their birthday. She was a Methodist instead of a New Believer, but Charles Thomas liked her anyways.

"I reckon so," Charles Thomas said, studying the sky.

"And just what brings you visitin this morning, Mr. Charles Thomas?"

"Mr. Rooster inside thare, Miss Barb?"

"Arta be. He been workin on that kitchen floor a' mine so long people acts like he lives hyare."

Without another word, Charles Thomas continued up the path towards Miss Barb's front door.

"Holt'er right thare, Charles Thomas." He turned and saw Miss Barb glaring with a smile and pointing down at his feet. "You think yer goin in my new kitchen muddy as all that?"

Charles Thomas looked down. Mud and grass clippings were plastered all over his feet and calves. Miss Barb took up her watering can and slowly, carefully rinsed his feet and legs, even rubbing between his little toes to rid them of any stubborn mud. When she was satisfied, she took off the bandana she wore to cover her hair and she dried his feet just as gentle as can be. When she'd finished he thanked her solemnly and then headed up her front steps. Miss Barb gave him a little pat on the butt before he escaped her reach.

Rooster was laying there on the new kitchen floor when Charles Thomas came in. He was curled up on his side, looking for all the world like a giant, hairy, new-born baby, grunting as he scooted along the wall with a paint brush in one hand and a paper cup half-full of white paint in the other. Charles Thomas stood there for a while without Rooster looking up from his work.

Layin on the floor like that with his buttcrack showin seems a strange thing fer the Lord Amighty to be doin! Charles Thomas's Prayer Voice spoke so loud that

Charles Thomas looked around to make sure nobody'd heard.

Maybe this is one a' them mysterious ways a' workin that everbody always talks about Him doin? Charles Thomas hissed back in his head.

Then Miss Maggie, his Sunday School teacher popped up saying, *Who are we to question the Lord's Will?*

And then he heard the Visitin Preacher saying in that funny voice of his: *Knock on that door. Ask and it will be given to you!*

So, Charles Thomas cleared his throat like a man and said, "What ye doin thare, Mr. Rooster?"

Rooster glanced over.

"What ye say thare, Charles Thomas? It's been a wet[11]."

Charles Thomas nodded. Rooster's eyes were red as the morning sun.

"Me, I'm paintin this hyare baseboard so I can get me a check and finally get on outa hyare."

"Ye ain't been hyare no time, iye[12] Mr. Rooster?" Charles Thomas said.

---

11 'It's been a wet': It's been a while.

12 'Iye': Corruption of 'is you'. In Common American English this would be 'have you' or, in other contexts, 'do you have', for example: "Iye got any crabs?"

"Damn if I don't get it from all sides," Rooster moaned before setting off on a tirade about why the job was taking so long and whose fault was what. All the while he kept on wriggling and grunting along the wall with his paintbrush. He reminded Charles Thomas of a worm inching along the edge of a bait can, trying to find his way out before your hand reaches down to put him on a hook.

In the middle of the brand-new linoleum was a can of white paint on a square of blue tarp. Charles Thomas went over to investigate while Rooster's speech wound down.

After Rooster ran out of steam, he glanced over at Charles Thomas again.

"Hooo-wee! Look at that cast yer got. 'Zit true what I'm heard 'bout you jumpin off a' RJ's ruff?'"

Charles Thomas was pleased that Rooster knew the story, and he turned to hide his blushing face.

"Yeuh, I was testin a parachute for RJ and Mikey Jr. and Boogie-3."

"Lord, ain't you smart[13]," Rooster scoffed.

"Been smart 'nough if them boys made a parachute that was worth a dern."

[13] A prime example of Johnsontown backspeak.

Rooster's laugh exploded, filling the kitchen with hacks and coughs.

After a minute Rooster came crawling over to the paint can in the middle of the room. He refilled his paper cup without spilling a drop, and then he crawled back to the wall and resumed his scooting and dabbing. Charles Thomas decided to focus on opening his heart to see if anything might happen. But again he got lost in the image of chopping his heart in two like a ripe tomato and the insides going everywhere.

After a bit Rooster said, "You come clear up hyare just ta watch me work?"

Charles Thomas probed his finger down into the cast where it hurt and itched. Then he said, "See, it's 'cause I'm got me this busted arm, and I cain't hardly do nothin." He squatted by the paint can and rapped the knuckles of his good hand on the floor like the men on the island did when they were asking a favor. "Cain't go swimmin, nor ride a bike, nor play ball, nor nothin."

"That's one a' them things yer got ta think about 'fore you do a fool-ass thing like jumpin off a ruff just 'cause them older boys tolt ye to. Ye might just learn a lesson outa all this!"

Charles Thomas chose to ignore that. He dipped his index finger into the white paint. It came back coated like it was dressed in a dripping cloud. He studied the drips awhile, and then he wiped his finger on his fiery red swimming trunks.

"Mr. Rooster, 'zit true yer a carpenter?"

"I'm been called worse."

"Weretn't Jesus a carpenter, too?"

"So I'm heardt."

"And ye fix things?"

"Yeah, purty much anything that's broke I can fix'er."

Charles Thomas felt his pulse quicken, but he kept his emotions in check. After a bit he said, casual as he could, "Whatye think a' miracles Mr. Rooster?"

"Sheeeww, I think I'm done one hell of a miracle on Barb's rotted-ass kitchen floor hyare. And Calhoon and Booger Jr. and Earl Sr. is makin jokes 'bout how they's puttin bets on if I finish or die first and all that. Well, I'ma tell ye one thing, I like'ta see any swingin dingaling on this island come up hyare and do what I'm done in this hyare kitchen!"

Once Rooster got started grumbling and complaining it was awful hard to stop him.

The truth was Charles Thomas couldn't believe his luck. A miracle floor! Fantasies unspooled like a ball of yarn bouncing down steps. He imagined his cast instantly gone, his arm pain-free and himself free as a bird. For a few seconds he allowed himself to imagine what it would be like if his Father came back to the island like Christ from the clouds. Heavenly music. Beams of sunlight. He was almost too pleased to bear it.

Meanwhile, Rooster was ranting on and on. Charles Thomas's eyes fell on a second paper cup and a pair of brushes. He thought maybe if he stayed and gave Rooster a hand, Rooster might just fix him up. Anyways Charles Thomas liked the idea of working side by side with the old man. He envisioned how it would be: the two of them passing the whole day together. Saw them straightening up at the end of the day to look at their work. Rooster would put his hand on Charles Thomas's shoulder and say, *Charles Thomas, dern if ye ain't 'bout the best painter I'm ever seen. A daggone artist is what ye are.*

Art class is one a' my best grades, Charles Thomas would say modestly.

Well, I tell you what. Just 'cause yer done so great I'll fix ye up.

Rooster would snap his fingers and the cast and the pain would disappear. (Cue heavenly music and beams of sunlight.)

Charles Thomas hefted up the surprisingly heavy paint can. He had to use the fingers of his broken arm to grip the handle and his good arm to tilt the bottom of the can over the cup. The paint began to flow, but then, all at once, the weight of the paint hit the side of the paper cup, and the cup tipped over. White paint moved like silent lava across the new floor, spreading out as quick and thick as sin.

Rooster didn't seem to notice and continued wriggling and grunting and grumbling along the wall. Charles Thomas spotted a roll of paper towels by Miss Barb's sink. He hoisted himself up onto the counter – a shot of pain spiking up his arm – and grabbed the roll. When he looked back he saw that his bare feet had tracked a trail of paint across the floor, and his hands had left prints across the new counter top.

Rooster looked up.

"Jesus-Fuckin-Christ, you little Shit!" Rooster dropped his cup and brush, stumbling to his feet and pulling at his hair. Paint was everywhere. Before Rooster could take two steps, Charles Thomas sprang down off the counter and was tracking white paint out the door. He bolted past Miss Barb, who was straightening up in her garden and looking confused, and he was out the front gate and sprinting eastward along Sun Street by the time Rooster got to the doorway, hollering: "You little Basterd! I'ma be hyare another week just cleanin up yer Gawddamned mess, you little Shit!"

Charles Thomas knew that running was wicked and weak, and that it was going to make everything worse, but it was like the Devil was in his legs and he just couldn't stop. Rooster was the old school type of disciplinarian who'd whup your butt with anything close at hand, and he'd had an awful violent look in his eye, so Charles Thomas figured it was best just to find somewhere to lay low for now. He could pretty well imagine that Rooster was gonna get in his truck and drive all around the island until he found Charles Thomas – or his Mom – and then Rooster would rant and rave and maybe whup Charles Thomas in the middle of the street until he cried in front of everyone. And then Charles Thomas would probably be stuck in the house the rest of the summer or maybe more. So Charles Thomas ran – knowing it was wrong, but doing it just the same – his bare feet slapping the hot asphalt and smarting like tacks were being driven up through his calloused soles.

He felt like his whole day was ruined, like his whole summer was ruined, and like his arm might just be broke forever. And the running just made his arm throb all the worse, like it was set to split the cast. He thought he might cry, but then he imagined the older boys mocking him; RJ's voice singing, *Big Crybaby Charles Thomikins, cry baby cry.* He imagined his Uncle Furry shaking his head at Big Crybaby Charles Thomas and being embarrassed all over to be his uncle, and so Charles Thomas swallowed his tears and just focused on the hurt of his arm and his feet smacking the road.

But (Lord forgive him) Damn it All! It had seemed so close! For a moment, there on the kitchen floor, it had seemed like Rooster was The One, like his miracles were as good as worked. And then, out of nowhere, an accident had to ruin it all.

His Prayer Voice came to him then, speaking like what his Uncle Furry always said: *Just remember: God has a plan.*

But why'd God hafta let me get that close just to ruin it all? Charles Thomas demanded back. His Prayer Voice didn't have an answer to that, the big phony. But then Charles Thomas had the consoling thought that Rooster probably wasn't Jesus anyhow, because Jesus wouldn't call you a little Shit, nor take His own name in vain now, would He? So maybe Jesus was just there waiting to be found yet. Charles Thomas felt his flame glint a little brighter, and he paused like a stunned bird, only half knowing where he was on his own island.

His feet had led him south down Haven Hill, and immediately he realized he was right beside the perfect place to hide: Oldman Trinks's graveyard. Charles Thomas liked Oldman Trinks's graveyard because it was nearly always quiet and shady, and because it was surrounded on three sides by a wall of honeysuckle and vines that made it seem enchanted like an overgrown castle.

It was Oldman Trinks's graveyard because it was behind Oldman Trinks's house, and Oldman Trinks took care of the graves. He cut the grass and kept the honeysuckle and vines from invading. Everybody in Oldman Trinks's graveyard had been dead for like a hundred years or more. They all had the same last names as everybody Charles Thomas knew on the island – Parks, Pinder, Butchard, Callahan, Reed and Stokes – but then they had these strange first names like Cephas, Nedra, Eleazer, or Nicodemus that made you think that they'd stepped right out the Old Testament.

Charles Thomas passed the firehouse and awkwardly hopped a couple fences – pain shooting up his broke arm each time – and then scrambled through a hedge and he was there inside. Safe. He collapsed, panting, onto one of the low concrete caps that they put on all the island graves so that the bodies don't come floating up in a hurricane tide.

He lay there for a while with the concrete cooling his back. His chest was heaving and his ears were thudding, and he spread his good arm and his bad arm wide like he was trying to embrace the trees and the sky and everything. He closed his eyes, and the sound of the locusts roosting in the graveyard's bushes and trees swelled inside his head like they were accusing him. He'd sinned; that was for sure. He'd known what he'd done was wrong – especially the running away – but he'd done it anyhow. The locusts' chorus swelled and swelled, and suddenly behind his pinched lids he imagined one locust, big as a Rottweiler, coming at him, gnashing its fangs all set to eat his sinning soul. Charles Thomas panicked.

Repent! his Prayer Voice hollered, *Repent all that paint and that runnin away! And don't think I forgot that D-word ye slipped in thare!*

Charles Thomas knew it was repent now or have his arm broke forever. That and not being chosen on that Final Day, and being eaten by giant locusts. His Father gone forever.

I'm Sorry, God, he cried out in his mind, *I'm Sorry, Jesus. I'm sorry for the paint, and for runnin away and for cussin and for everthing I do wrong all the time and fer all my sins.*

No sooner had he finished his prayer than the locusts' chanting abruptly ceased.

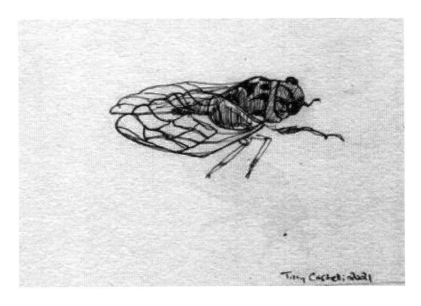

His Prayer Voice nodded its head saying, *God's forgivingness is what that is.*

In that brief silence, Charles Thomas's ears picked up a rustle and a sniffle, and he sat up just as shocked as Lazarus.

He had assumed he was alone in the graveyard, but there, in the darkest, most-overgrown corner, was a lonely island girl named Dolores, crying silently and watching Charles Thomas through her fingers. Dolores had two dolls and a pink plastic tea set on top of one of the graves' concrete caps. Charles Thomas's first thought was that it was strange that he'd come in the graveyard without seeing Dolores, but then he thought: *No, that's just Dolores, just a girl ye ain't really notice none.*

He got up and went over to her and sat on the nearest grave. He didn't say anything for a minute; he just picked at the crumbly concrete cap he was sitting on. Dolores kept hidden in her hands. She was three years older than Charles Thomas. That, and her being a girl – a quiet one at that – made the situation pretty awkward. Her blonde hair was jumbled about everywhere and tangled like a bird's nest. Her knees were stained with dirt and grass. She had a faded blue dress on, and where her skin showed it was so pale it looked blue, like he was looking straight through her to her blue blood beneath the skin.

At last he said, "How come yer cryin, Dolores?"

Dolores buried her face deeper in her hands and just said, "Go away," quiet as a butterfly.

"You cryin 'cause yer playin all alone?"

"Sole was hyare, but she left 'cause I tolt'er I wanted to be alone."

Sole was Dolores's younger sister, a year older than Charles Thomas.

"But how come yer cryin then?"

Her voice was suddenly full and fierce:

"Just 'cause I feel like it, okay! That good 'nough fer ye?"

Her pale shoulders bobbed up and down in her tangled hair as she sobbed on quietly.

Charles Thomas thought a moment about that strange idea of crying just because you felt like it. Then he told her, "Me, I ain't cried since I was six year old." He hoped that would impress Dolores and make her stop. "My Uncle Furry tolt me last time I cried, he said 'Yer the man a' the house now. Yer got to quit all that spit[14]! A man, he don't cry,' Furry says."

Dolores lowered her hands at last and laid her sharp blue eyes on Charles Thomas like he was something for sale that wasn't worth the price.

[14] 'Spit': Another of the islander's substitute curse words.

"Dern if that ain't the most common[15] thing I'm heardt in all my life."

It didn't much matter what she said. Charles Thomas could tell he had cheered her up a bit, but still, she didn't look properly impressed. His Prayer Voice came rumbling into his head saying: *Time to pull out the big guns, Charles Thomas!*

So he told her: "I ain't even cried when I broke this hyare arm," holding up his neon-orange cast like a trophy.

Dolores didn't look impressed in the slightest. She just wiped her nose on the back of her dirty hand and said, soft as can be, "'Magine you cry all the time when they ain't nobody lookin."

The truth of that drove a nail right through the boy. He hated to admit it, even to himself, but sometimes some stupid idea would get stuck in his head, like how it'd be if his Father were there to take him out on the water like other boys' dads did, or practice his hitting or whatever, and then, when he thought like that, he'd have to hide himself away where nobody was watching and cry until the idea went away. He felt his face burn, like she'd caught him naked, and he heard that Voice in his head crying out for revenge. He knew that Dolores was eleven or so because

15 'Common': Foolish or crass

she'd graduated from Jtown Elementary in a big ceremony just a week before, and was going to The Big School in Cambridge[16] that next fall, and so he said,

"Ain't you too old to be havin tea parties in the graveyard anyhow?"

His comment had the intended effect: Dolores rushed into tears again. Charles Thomas immediately regretted that he'd said it at all.

"Aww, I'm sorry... Come on now..."

She wailed on. He felt helpless.

"Dolores, I tell you what, I, I ... I'll tell you a secret if you quit yer cryin."

"I don't wanna hear no kinda secret yer got," she sobbed.

"Yer gonna like it. I swear." He saw that the sobs were mostly theater now, and that those fragile blue eyes were half-watching him through her boney fingers. "I might even let ye come along with me," he said to seal the deal.

---

[16] Johnsontown has managed, against all odds, to continue hanging onto its tiny elementary school even though the school averages less than 40 students at any given time. Once children reach 6th grade they must then take the 22-mile bus ride to 'The Big School' in Cambridge. Cambridge Middle has 533 students, more than the entire population of Johnsontown. Cambridge MD is the County Seat of Dorchester County, population 12,326, a veritable metropolis in the eyes of islanders.

Dolores lowered her hands. "And where 'zactly do ye think yer goin at?"

Charles Thomas let the silence work on her. The locusts in the trees hummed like a motor. Finally, just when he felt he was going to lose her, he said, "I'm lookin to find Jesus tday."

Dolores's face remained blank. She was a Methodist girl, but she was from a respected Methodist family. Her grandpappy was a church elder and her mummum played the keyboard for the choir and helped run the Methodist oyster suppers every winter at the firehouse. Everybody liked the oyster suppers. Charles Thomas was confident that Dolores would understand.

"You mean like to save yer soul?" she asked, her face locked on his. Charles Thomas realized for the first time that she was kinda pretty.

"Yeah, well that too. But really I'm lookin to track Him down so's to see if He can fix this hyare busted arm I'm got."

He decided it was best not to mention the part about raising the dead. His Prayer Voice commended Charles Thomas's sound judgment.

For a second Dolores's swollen eyes remained blank, and then a terrible look of understanding broke across her face. "You mean like yer lookin for Jesus, like He's hyare on the island?"

She studied his eyes, and then she started giggling in a silent way and covering her face again.

"Charles Thomas, Jesus, He been dead fer like a thousand years or sumptin like that."

Charles Thomas felt again like he was naked before her, and he felt the urgent need to flee just as certain as if a lion were at his heels. He didn't think a second more, he just ran – out from the graveyard, out through Oldman Trinks's front yard, and out into the street – all the while with that quiet giggle of Dolores's chasing after him.

He broke out into Haven Hill and sprinted south. The sun was blasting down on the street, and the heat seemed to be squeezing him like it wanted to turn him into nothing. After a bit he stopped in the shade of a fig tree near the end of Haven Hill. The blood pounded in his head, and the locusts chanted so loud he could feel them in his throat. The flame in his spirit was all but out. His eyes got leaky. RJ and the older boys swarmed in his head with a hum of insults. But then he thought he'd be dernt if he was gonna let some girl like Dolores make him cry in the middle of the street, with who-knows-who watching.

His Prayer Voice ranted and raved inside his head, saying: *Stupid know-it-all Dolores, actin like she knowed everything, like everybody else is a idiot. What did a dernt Methodist girl know anyhow? Ain't that Visitin Preacher said Jesus was hyare on the island, and it was yer mission to find Him? Ain't he said you hadta find Jesus fer yerself? And now, here's Dolores laughin in yer face fer doin just like that Visitin Preacher said! What the heck does dumb, lonely, borin, cryin, little Dolores know compared to a Visitin Preacher that people come from all over to see and hear?*

Charles Thomas's Prayer Voice ranted on, but despite all the reassurances, doubt came flooding in around him like a rising tide. Maybe he was just a stupid, foolish kid and there was no Jesus to be found, and his arm was gonna be broke forever, and his Father was gone and good as dead just like his Mom said. Tears bubbled up again.

But then, Charles Thomas thought about it hard and put his head on straight and walked out into the sun again. People on the island did say all the time that Jesus lived, and they all talked about Him just like He was somebody you'd invite to supper. Everybody talked like they knew Him: about what He liked and what He knew and stuff. 'Jesus loves good little boys,' his Mom would tell him, or,

'Good Lord knows I ain't got a cent to squeeze.' When times were good she'd say, 'Lord Jesus woked up smilin tday,' or, when Charles Thomas did something bad she'd say, 'Jesus is shakin His head at ye now." Charles Thomas knew you didn't talk like that about someone that had been dead a thousand years. Heck, people didn't even talk like that about his Father, and he'd only been gone five years. Charles Thomas kicked a soda can along the street. Stupid, know-it-all Dolores. He focused on how he hated her, and all the nasty things he could do to her. He kicked that can and imagined tying Dolores up to a waterbush and leaving her out in the marsh to get sucked dry by the skeeters. The flame in his spirit burned a little brighter thinking like that.

"Charles Thomas Parks! Pick ye up that thare can!" an old black lady's voice screeched out suddenly from a shaded porch.

He kicked it again.

"Charles Thomas!"

"It ain't mine," he called to the empty street.

"I'on't care who's it'tiz; you kickt'er, so you pick'er up."

Charles Thomas didn't move.

"Certain as the Gospel-Truth," the rusty, old voice hollered, "I'll go me right hyare an' now an' find yer mother, Margrit Lanney Price-Parks, an' I'll make her make ye pick'er up if I'm got to."

Charles Thomas crushed the can and put it in his pocket. The street was getting too hot to walk in anyhow. Tide was down and out of the island's ditches on the higher ground of Haven Hill, and there was plenty of nice, soft, black mud cooking in the sun. Charles Thomas plodded around in the mud for a while, pretending he was leaving behind fossilized prints like a dinosaur, doing his best not to think about Dolores. The mud was hot and thick, just right for Dino mud. A pair of shrieking gulls circled: pterodactyls. Charles Thomas was one of those cavemen that had to kill dinosaurs with nothing but a spear. But God had made him into a Super Caveman. He spun a long stick like a Ninja Caveman and stabbed, stabbed, stabbed into the heart of a huge T. Rex, saving RJ who was tied to a tree and about to be eaten. RJ was very grateful.

Thank ye thare Super Caveman Charles Thomas. Sorry I called you a Crybaby. Wanna come over and play PS4? I got a buncha sweet games that yer Mom won't let ye play. And Hot Pockets.

I guess so. But just for the record RJ: I play what I want.

My bad C.T. I know yer right.

The boy's nose started itching then. He knew that meant someone, somewhere was talking about him. Then Charles Thomas caught sight of a pair of crabbers pedaling up Haven Hill, fresh in off the water and still in their orange bibs and white rubber boots. They spotted him at a distance, and the older of the two, Dookie, who was somehow kin, called, "What ye say thare Cousin Charles Thomas?"

Charles Thomas stared down at the primordial mud, fearful that word of the sin he'd left behind on Miss Barb and Mr. Bill's floor had spread to the men. He felt the locusts throbbing like they were in his head.

"If it ain't Charles 'Paratrooper' Parks," the other man, Ding-Dong John, yodeled into the listening street. "Hey thare Trooper, how 'bout ye come on by the house when yer free…" Ding-Dong paused to stretch out his joke, and then chortled, "I'm got me a parachute needs testin!"

Both men erupted for all the world to hear. Their laughs and the creaking of their bikes faded away up Haven Hill. Charles Thomas kept staring at the mud until they disappeared so as to hide the blush seeping across his face. But, funny enough, he found himself grinning too, knowing those watermen were all talking about him. The fame felt good in a way.

The other thing that made Charles Thomas smile was he knew that if Dookie and Ding-Dong were just getting in off the water that meant it was 10:30 or 11. And that meant that the County Dock was the place to be, what with all the watermen unloading their crabs, docking their boats and getting cleaned up. And Uncle Furry would be getting in and probably have a piece of time to talk.

Charles Thomas headed south down the last chunk of Haven Hill and then turned east onto Wilkens Avenue. The Creek opened up before him there at the end of Wilkens, shinning like the Promised Land. His problem now was crossing the gauntlet of Callahan's Family Store[17] and its perpetual group of islanders chatting out front.

There were two separate groups in the street out front of Callahan's. Charles Thomas scanned their faces for his Mom, or Rooster, or Miss Barb, or anyone else that might be keen to wring him out. In the first group were

---

[17] Callahan's Family Store is an 80-year-old institution. Run by Bill Callahan Sr. and his wife, Miss Joan, Callahan's is the last general store left on the island. (There were nearly a dozen stores on the island in its heyday.) On its shelves you can find everything from bread and produce, to fishing supplies, motor oil, bottom paint, and the ubiquitous white-rubber watermen's boots. Two things you will not find there are alcohol or cigarettes because Miss Joan is a devout Methodist who refuses to support the vices of others. At any time between 4 a.m. when the store opens until 4 p.m. when it closes, Callahan's is filled with gossiping islanders, making it the beating heart of day-to-day island social life.

some dingey, old Methodists that Charles Thomas figured would likely leave him be. However, the second group was more problematic: Rooster's best friend Calhoon Greenhawk and Calhoon's sometime-girlfriend, Marsha Pinder, were there talking to two rich-looking strangers, who Charles Thomas figured to be tourists. He approached until he could hear Calhoon's gravelly storytelling voice, and then hung there in the shade, calculating on how he might could get by unscathed.

Charles Thomas loved Calhoon, and he loved listening to Calhoon talk from his bottomless bag of wild island tales and legends. The problem was, of course, there was a chance that Calhoon would try and take Charles Thomas back to Rooster, to face Rooster's vengeance, whatever that may be. Calhoon was a drunk, everybody knew that, and Charles Thomas could see a big can in a paper bag that Calhoon was half-hiding behind his back. Church folk didn't think much of Calhoon, but Charles Thomas loved him anyways. Calhoon's shaggy hair was bald on top like a monk's, and his face looked like a muppet's 'cause his features were so red and swollen.

Calhoon's on/off girlfriend Marsha stood there swaying like she couldn't stand still and laughing in the two tourists' faces. It was near impossible to get to the age of eight on the island and not have heard the word 'whore' and Marsha's name yoked together. Even sweetest and most conservative of New Believer women were prone to say, casual as hanging laundry, 'Ye heardt who that whore Marsha's been layin wit now?' In fact, when Charles Thomas heard Reverend A.D. or his Sunday School teacher, Miss Maggie, talking about Jesus 'hangin round sinners and lost souls,' Marsha and Calhoon were pretty much the faces he imagined. Marsha was skinny and bent-looking like rusty wire, and she and Calhoon didn't have a dozen rotten teeth to share between them. They were both smoking like always as Calhoon told his story to the extremely confused and uncomfortable tourist couple.

Charles Thomas knew Calhoon's story well. It was about a fight between one of the watermen, who had just passed on his bike – Dookie, the one who was somehow kin – and a black feller named Cann who'd slept with Dookie's wife, Jude. Charles Thomas knew that there wasn't much worse on the island than sleeping with someone's wife, especially if it was a black feller and a white woman, even if he couldn't ever figure what about sleeping could be all that bad.

Calhoon was saying, "You can 'magine when Dookie fount out he was hotter'an hellfire. Me, I was with him, an' a bunch a' us went up thare to Sun Street where most a' the blacks an' Cann lives at. Dookie had a bottle a' Popov in'im, and he weretn't thinkin none too right. So he started to bangin on Cann's door, screamin all 'maginable, til every kitchen light on the street come on, an' Cann come limpin out the door just as big an' black as night. See Cann's got him "a disability" (Calhoon finger quoted) ever since him an' Gerty got in that car wreck that night near Bucktown when they was three-sheets an' hidin out from Gerty's husband, Newt. Cann's got him a cane and disability checks, an' everything. The first thing Dookie done was kick that cane so Cann had to grab at the rail to keep from goin ass over tin cup. Next thing Dookie starts hollerin right in Cann's face 'bout, 'Who does Cann think he is, screwin 'round with his wife,' and how, 'He don't never want to hear another word-one 'bout Cann an' Jude again,' and then Dookie says low-like, 'In the good ol' days we'd a' all played dress up an' took ye fer a walk in the marsh, Boy.'

"Wooo, Lord, that's what it took. Next thing we knowed Cann had busted Dookie right up under the chin and knocked Dook clean up over the rail, clear off the porch, an' into the flower garden, an' by time we looked up Cann was gone in that house, just quick as a jackrabbit, like he ain't never needed no cane a-tall." Calhoon laughed, clapping the man-tourist on the back. "Now ye ever seent a thing like that Mitch?!" he bellowed. "Shoot we ain't knowed what in Hell to do, what with all them quiet, black faces watchin from behind kitchen windders. And then Rooster started crackin up, an' we all got to laughin fit to raise Christ, an' we got Dookie up – him not hardly knowin whare he was at, nor what happened. And Dookie, he just kept sayin, 'Whare, whare, whare'd he go at?'" Calhoon threw back his head in a laugh like an earthquake. "Long yarn short, see that's how come I hollert what I'm hollert when ol' Dook come by on his bike."

The tourist couple seemed utterly lost, looking around like they were searching for a glowing EXIT sign.

"No, we ain't got no characters to know on this island," Calhoon said shaking his head before he closed his eyes and tipped back his bald crown to take a long swig from his paper bag.

Charles Thomas saw his opportunity. He darted out quick as a snake on the other side of the street, but sure enough, Calhoon spotted him and hollered, "Charles 'Paratrooper' Parks! Come on over hyare. I'm got ta buy ye a Cokey Coler!"

Marsha cackled that metallic laugh of hers until she hacked up something that she then spit on the ground. At the sound of the words Cokey Coler, Charles Thomas realized that he'd had a powerful thirst for a right good while, and he thought he might as well stick around and listen to Calhoon until the Coke was produced; Calhoon didn't sound like he was working for the hand of justice anyhow. So Charles Thomas walked over and joined the four of them. The man-tourist stuck out his hand in Calhoon's direction and said, "Well, it sure was nice meeting you... Calvin was it?"

Calhoon ignored the man's hand and said, "Holt up now, Mitch, Sherry, yer got ta hear this! Charles Thomas hyare is Johnsontown's amateur skydiving champion," (Marsha cackled and hacked) "and he was up thare this morning, to Barb an' Bill Pinder's, where Rooster's been puttin down that kitchen floor fer a coon's age, an' ol' Paratrooper Parks hyare, he dumpt out a whole Fuckin gallon a' white paint 'crost Rooster's brand-new Gawddamed floor." Calhoon busted out in his earth-shaking laugh. "Now what ye make a' that, Mitch?" he bellowed, slapping the man-tourist on the shoulder with that bear paw of his.

The man-tourist opened his mouth like a fish gulping air.

Calhoon went on irregardless: "See now, Charles Thomas hyare, he's hittin fer the home team, 'cause me an' Earl Sr. in thare," (Calhoon gestured over his shoulder to Callahan's) "and Booger Jr. an' a few other boys from the poker table got to bettin on if Rooster'd finish that-thare floor a' Barb an' Bill's or if he'd die first, and me, I'm got my money on Rooster takin the long dirt nap – I love'im dearly, but it's a sure bet – *hakhahahakk* – and see, Charles Thomas hyare done put Rooster in the hornets nest tday, and, he probly done drove Rooster's blood pressure through the ruff. So I figger I owe Trooper Parks hyare a Cokey Coler, huh Mitch?" Again Calhoon released that roar of a laugh and thumped the man-tourist's shoulder.

Charles Thomas stood on one foot and then the other when the asphalt got too hot to stand. In that brutal heat his thirst seemed unbearable, like he was drying up like a little puddle. His Prayer Voice was hollering for him to get out the street where Rooster or someone else might come along to punish him at any moment. But, Charles Thomas knew Calhoon wasn't done toying with the tourists yet, and his thirst was awful powerful, so Charles Thomas stuck around and asked:

"Uncle Furry come by yet Mr. Calhoon?"

"I ain't seent him," Calhoon replied leaning on the man-tourist like a fence post.

"Dookie and Ding-Dong John come by a piece ago." Marsha volunteered.

"Yeah I'm seent 'em too." Charles Thomas said. "They done awright tday?"

"Lord knows they ain't nare a decent basket[18] ta be foundt out thare right now," Calhoon said shaking his head.

"Hot as she is, it ain't no suprise," Charles Thomas said.

Marsha and Calhoon nodded in agreement.

"Peeler pottin's[19] been out, too," Marsha added. "Pop-pop Terkle said he ain't put but a pair a' boxes[20] on the truck this morning, an' most of 'em Mediums and Hotels[21] at that."

---

[18] 'A basket' refers to a bushel basket, the standard of measurement for crabs and oysters on the Bay. In most other parts of the Bay this is commonly referred to simply as a bushel, but for whatever reason everyone on Jtown inverted the abbreviation making it 'a basket'.

[19] 'Peeler pottin': A specific form of crabpot used to catch 'peelers' or molting crabs. Instead of the standard hardcrab pot that uses dead fish as bait, a 'peeler pot' uses a 'buffalo jimmy' (a clawless mature male crab) to lure in mate-seeking female peeler crabs. These peelers are then taken to peeler floats where within a few days they will become soft crabs.

[20] 'A box': The standard for selling live soft-shell crabs. 24 crabs to a box.

"They ain't nare a thing to know 'bout a jimmy[22] 'cept he comes, he goes, and he bites." Calhoon said with unarguable certainty. "They'll be back soon as they's good an' ready," he said.

Marsha and Charles Thomas nodded their assent.

The woman-tourist was tugging on her husband's sleeve to extract him from Calhoon's lean.

"Actually, I think we've really got to get going. It was very nice talking to you, but we haven't got much time and..."

Calhoon swung around on them, and this time he dropped his hands on both their shoulders. "Yer a poor pair ye are: you two must be just lost in the pea-soup[23]. 'Tween the accent, the names, everbody knowin everbody, and all them words ye ain't never heardt afore," he looked down at them as if they were his own lost lambs, "Mitch, you got any idear what in the Hell we talkin 'bout?"

"Something about crabs?"

Calhoon and Marsha exploded.

---

[21] 'Mediums and Hotels': This refers to sizes of 'softies'. From smallest to biggest 'softies' are referred to as 'Mediums', 'Hotels', 'Primes', 'Jumbos', and 'Whales'. Each larger size fetches a higher price. Without these footnotes it is safe to assume our tourist couple might as well be listening to a foreign language.

[22] 'Jimmy': A mature male crab.

[23] 'Lost in the pea soup': This can be translated to 'lost in the fog' A thick fog is referred to as 'thick as pea soup,' thus this expression.

"Gawddamn ye ain't so lost as ye looked!"

Tears of laughter were climbing over the cliff of Calhoon's saggy eyes. He was staring off westward down the length of Wilkens, and then of a sudden, Calhoon's attention was yanked away to the lanky form of Raymond Hooper limping eastward towards them, his mean, black mutt Romeo at his heels. Marsha saw Raymond too, and it was like Charles Thomas and the tourists ceased to exist. Mitch and Sherry looked around blinking like some inconceivable miracle had saved them from Satan himself, and they booked it, probably for their car, to lock the doors and flee this island of heathens as fast as their Prius could take them away. No one except for Charles Thomas noted their exodus. Once Raymond got within earshot Calhoon hollered, "No, you 'on't know how'ta keep nobody waitin none!"[24]

Raymond didn't say a word or even change his step; he just kept limping towards them slow and steady as the hands on a clock. Everybody on the island knew Raymond Hooper was the island pharmacy. When Raymond finally reached them he eyed Charles Thomas up and down and

---

[24] Classic Johnsontown backspeak: 'You are habitually late.' Note the quadruple negative used for emphasis.

then said, "Come on Calhoon. Let's go 'round back," and abruptly Charles Thomas was left alone with Marsha.

Marsha followed the two men like her soul had gone with them and just her body was left behind to suffer. She picked at a scab near her nose until a little blossom of blood formed. She looked so hollow and trapped that Charles Thomas immediately thought of saving her like Princess Leia or Rapunzel or one of them other princesses.

He stared up into the lifeless leather of her face. He pictured Marsha all dressed in white like a bride, a bunch of flowers in her hands and her face magically younger. He imagined leading her into New Believers and seeing Jesus up front with the microphone. Jesus was very big with a huge beard like Charles Thomas's Uncle Furry, but with paler skin and those eyes that were identical to Charles Thomas's. The whole island was there like a wedding or a funeral. Jesus took the mic from its bracket and walked toward Marsha and Charles Thomas.

"*Great job thare, Charles Thomas,*" He'd say, "*Everbody give Charles Thomas a round of applause; he done saved Marsha.*"

Everybody would clap and cheer and then Charles Thomas would say:

"*No problem Jesus. That's what I do.*"

"Yer a good man, Charles Thomas. Yer gonna be rich an' famous. A savior on this island. I tell ye what: I'ma bring yer Father down hyare, an' we'll get that arm a' yers all fixed up. Whadaya say folks?"

More clapping in agreement.

"That'd be great, Jesus. Thanks a bunch."

Imagining it like that gave Charles Thomas some gumption. (Lord knows he needed some good points with Jesus.) He cleared his throat like a man and asked Marsha, "How come you don't never come to Church and try bein saved, Miss Marsha? It's fun. There's rock music and cupcakes and everthing else."

With what seemed like considerable effort Marsha swung her attention back around to Charles Thomas and reanimated herself. Her eyes moved all over his face and body like probing fingers. Then she cracked a smile.

"What, Charles Thomas? Them Bible-beaters send ye out fishin after lost souls? Huh?" She broke out into the same metallic, clacking laugh that she'd used on the tourists.

Charles Thomas felt his face light afire, but he kept on looking as solemn as he could. When the heat died down enough for him to talk normal he said, "But don't ye wanta save yer soul, Miss Marsha?"

Marsha's stony face softened like it had been moved by a spell, and she reached out her chunky fingers and touched Charles Thomas's chin just as gentle as the breeze. The smell of cigarettes enveloped him.

"Honey, I'm had me 'nough Church fer two lifetimes."

He could see her spirit moving inside of her.

"Anyhow, gettin saved in church ain't never really set right with me. How I see it: both them churches ain't nothing but a buncha fellers in stuffed suits, makin up whatever rules suits'em so they can judge you like they want." She was getting worked up. "Dern if both them churches don't do nothing but point the finger at us "sinners" an' bicker with each other, dividin this whole island all the more."

Marsha took a deep rattling breath to calm herself some. She glanced over her shoulder, but didn't take her cool fingers from Charles Thomas's chin. Then she set her watery blue eyes on his and said, "Me, I like to deal with my Lord one-on-one if ye know what I mean, Sugar."

Charles Thomas felt the excitement running through him and across his face, and he couldn't help it, and he couldn't hide it with Marsha holding his chin like that.

"You mean like ye *know* Jesus?"

He said it too quick, without care enough to keep the hope out of his voice, and after his question came out it hung there in the air as shameful as a fart. His mind writhed, and RJ's voice popped into his head saying, *You idiot! You stupid soundin fool!*

Marsha looked for a second like she wanted to bend down and pick him up – which was just the last thing Charles Thomas wanted. He thanked the Lord when she didn't, and then she told him quiet-like, as if it was a dear secret, "Not a day goes by that I don't talk with Him."

Charles Thomas felt his heart throbbing in his head beside his Prayer Voice and the pulse of the locusts in the bushes along the road. Again, it was like he could feel the cool key to his miracles nearly between his fingertips. He stared into Marsha's face, and those leathery lines seemed transfigured just soft as milk and full of knowing, like a smiling mother.

"And Jesus, He says things to you, too?" he asked at last.

"Honey, He'll talk to ye in a million ways if ye just know how to watch an' listen."

Charles Thomas felt the doubt that Dolores had flooded him with disappearing, like tide was running out and the sun was touching where all that water had been. His flame sprang up again within his soul.

Then Calhoon's voice came rumbling towards them like a wagon wheel.

"Gawddamn if them two tourist weretn't just as scairt as I don't know what!" he was saying to Raymond. "They ain't knowed whuther ta Shit er run!"

Marsha pulled her hand back and reversed her face to stone. Calhoon dropped his heavy hand on Charles Thomas's shoulder. Charles Thomas looked up into his face. It was grey and slack-looking like old meat. Raymond started limping back off again.

"Holt up now, Ray," Marsha called, forgetting Charles Thomas altogether and snatching at Raymond's T-shirt, "I know yer got yer own little honey pot. Lemme at least git a half 'fore ye go."

"I ain't got nare a thing for ye," Raymond said in an icy voice before limping off just like he'd come, leaving Marsha itchy and jittery as a rabbit that wants to run, and Calhoon swaying like he was dead on his feet. They'd both entirely forgotten that Charles Thomas was standing there. Calhoon's hand weighed upon Charles Thomas's shoulder lifeless as a boulder. Charles Thomas realized he wasn't getting a Cokey Coler, and he felt foolish for ever believing he would. But then, through the silence, his ears picked up the diesels rumbling in The Creek. He smelled the water calling him, and so he slipped out from under Calhoon's hand and made his leave with an unacknowledged "See ye all later" hanging in the air around poor Calhoon and Marsha's lost souls.

Charles Thomas felt a sudden urgency propelling him forward – the flame within him swelled and danced with all that Marsha'd said, and with the thought that his Uncle Furry was close at hand – and so he hustled eastward along Wilkens to where the pavement abruptly ended at the water's edge and the County Dock began.

The County Dock was really three parallel piers, all stretching out a hundred foot or so into the dark, swiftly moving water of The Creek. It was where most island watermen tied up their workboats (or their skiffs, for the watermen that kept their boats at their crabhouses). Charles Thomas headed out Middle Dock where the most action was. The splintery, creosoted boards were broiling under his feet, and the sun's glare was made double by the water. First thing Charles Thomas noted was that the tide was rushing out strong against the pilings, giving the men a true force to fight against.

It was primetime in The Creek, and Charles Thomas stood there sucking it all up like a thirsty plant. Workboats were cruising in under The Bridge from the Bayside. The tea-colored water of The Creek was a potato patch of confused wakes, and the air was filled with a dozen groaning diesels, all rising and falling in pitch as the men maneuvered about.

Close by, Trip Trinks was backing *Lady B* hard into her shallow slip, throwing up a wall of muddy water that crashed against the shoreline's crumbling bulkhead. Some older kids – RJ, Mikey Jr., Lily and Boogie-3 – hollered and splashed in the water around an old crabhouse just a stone's throw from The Bridge. At the end of Middle Dock, Booger Jr. had *Second Chance* alongside the crab buyer's boat from Hoopers Island.

Charles Thomas could hear the men yammering and complaining as they passed their pitiful few baskets from one boat to the other. Ancient, near-blind Booger Sr. came flying through the middle of everything in his skiff, straight as an arrow through the confusion of wakes and moving boats to get a report on the day from his son, and to harass the crab buyer some.

Three boats – *Miss Jenny Lee*, *Rebel Yell*, and *Annie T* – idled in the middle of The Creek, their captains a'middle,

flicking their shifters and speeders[25] back and forth to hold their positions against the swirling force of the current as they waited for Booger, Jr. to finish with the crab buyer. They fought the current and guided their boats just as casual and routine as rolling out of bed and making coffee in the morning, all the while keeping up a ceaseless flow of jokes and jabs from boat to boat. Charles Thomas spotted his Uncle Furry already tying up in his slip on Northard Dock. Then he saw All-Day-Dean come roaring into the mouth of The Creek on *Mariah Ruth*, slowing only after he was through The Bridge and back in the midst of the flock. Charles Thomas knew that All-Day was nearly always the last in The Creek. He did a quick inventory, figured everybody was back, and then he walked around to his Uncle Furry on Northard Dock.

---

[25] 'A'middle, flicking their shifters and speeders': The traditional Chesapeake Bay workboat has a steering station along the warshboard (see footnote 32) near the middle of the boat with a 'shifter' (a gear shift), a 'speeder' (the throttle), and often a steering stick connected to the rudder or else a helm which serves the same purpose.

Furry was standing in the stern of his chunky deadrise[26] *Leviathan*, cleaning half a bushel of lemons[27].

[26] 'Deadrise': The 'deadrise' – sometimes called a boxstern, or simply a workboat – is the great utilitarian Chesapeake Bay commercial fishing boat. Originally, of course, they were wood, though most have gone to fiberglass. They are characterized by a sharp bow that quickly transitions to a V shape moving aft along the hull to finish as a flat, shallow stern. There is a small cabin all the way forward, leaving the rest of the boat as an open cockpit/work area. Most are diesel powered and between 30 and 45 feet long. Workboats in the Chesapeake are almost exclusively painted white due to watermen's superstition that a boat of any other color is a disaster waiting to happen. The deadrise is an extremely versatile boat, used for crab potting, trotlining, oyster dredging, hand tonging and patent tonging, clamming, pound netting, gill netting, and more. The specific details of their design vary widely throughout the Chesapeake's many regions.

[27] 'Lemons': A female crab carrying fertilized eggs. The eggs come bursting out from her underside in a yellow ball with a sponge-like consistency giving this crab her other name: a 'sponge crab'. Law prohibits the harvest of these crabs because of their importance to the reproduction of the species.

Furry was a giant of a man. Every inch of visible skin was covered by coarse, dark hair except for a patch of face that shone like a bright red sun above his bushy beard. Furry didn't break from his work or acknowledge Charles Thomas in any way, but just the same Charles Thomas could feel that Furry knew he was there. Charles Thomas heard his uncle in his head saying, *A righteous man don't need to yack on all the time. His action's his word and his word's his action*, and so Charles Thomas kept quiet and watched.

Furry's gloved hands worked the crabs with the speed and efficiency of a machine designed for just that purpose and nothing else. He grabbed one squirming crab at a time from the basket at his hip. Then he ripped off the yellow, tennis ball-sized sack of eggs from her underside and tossed it in The Creek. Next he flipped the crab over, broke off her top shell, hosed out the guts and mustard[28], picking off the stubborn dead-man-fingers[29] before tossing the still moving crab into the basket with the others he'd already cleaned. Charles Thomas shifted over a bit closer so that he could peer down into the basket of already-

[28] 'Mustard': The yellow, liquidy fat within a crab.
[29] 'Dead-man-fingers': The gills of a crab, referred to as such because of their grey finger-like appearance.

cleaned lemons. They flipped around and clung to each other like they didn't know they were dead yet.

After waiting long enough Charles Thomas crouched and rapped his knuckles on the dock.

"Iye got any peelers fer me, Uncle Furry?"

Furry looked up at last and smiled, making his thick, sun-cooked face shine doubly from the dark mask of his hair and massive beard. His hands didn't cease for a second from their mechanical dance. His eyes were a soft brown, just like Charles Thomas's – just like the eyes above the supper table. With a familiar, jagged feeling Charles Thomas was reminded of that muddled memory of his own Father's face.

"Yeuh, I'm got a few peelers fer ye," Furry said, turning back to his lemons, "if ye can make supper outa them fat rock[30] that's all time nosin 'round hyare."

"That's fair," Charles Thomas said. He watched the blurry crosses that Furry had tattooed atop each forearm: the muscles rippled beneath the surface making the crosses

---

[30] 'Rock': The Striped Bass ('rock' or 'rockfish', as it's known in the Chesapeake) is an anadromous fish that can be found throughout the Atlantic coast from Canada to the Gulf states. It is characterized by a streamlined silver body marked with longitudinal black stripes and is prized by sport fishermen and restaurants alike. The largest recorded was 5.9 ft and 126 lbs, though the average size is between 5-32 lbs. They are well known for scavenging around crabhouses.

roll and shake with life. Water from the hose was caught in Furry's bushy arm hair. Each drop held the sun like jewels on the cross.

"You ain't 'posed to be keepin them lemons, iye Uncle Furry?"

Furry laughed and glanced up at Charles Thomas, his face full of good humor. "Cain't slip nothin by on ol' Charles Thomas."

"Them dernt water cops, they'll hit ye with a big ol' fine if they catches ye, won't they, Uncle Furry?"

"Don't I know it," Furry said shaking his head, "But Dink got ta tossin back so many dern purty crabs I couldn't hardly stand it." Furry tore off a yellow sack of eggs and held it up in the white sunlight. "They say this hyare is a hunert-thousand baby crabs, er sumptin like that. You 'magine if all them crabs was swimmin round? Huh? They'd be crawlin out the wuter an' conquerin the land! Huh?!" Furry broke out into a laugh like a roll of thunder. When it subsided he said, "Good Lord put us hyare keep'em in their place. Masters of all the beasts of the land an' of the sea."

Charles Thomas took that in and nodded his head. He imagined what the world would be like if there weren't watermen like his Uncle, if crabs ruled the earth. Crabs crawling all over the streets and sidewalks. Giant crabs straddling houses and using their car-sized claws to snap off telephone poles like they were pretzel rods. On that day him and Furry'd be there, wielding dual shotguns and firing from the hip, sending those crabs back to the watery Hell from where they come.

Furry's hands paused so he could sip from his can of Mountain Dew. There was a bucket of similar cans by Furry's heel. Charles Thomas felt his thirst consume him once again, but he was too proud to ask too many favors all at once. Furry went back to ripping the crabs apart. After a bit he held up a crab and said, "Don't expect yer Aunt Sally'll be none too pleased to see these hyare. I brought home two bushel last week an' Aunt Sally, she tolt me, 'Don't ye dare bring home a crab-one fer me to pick this next week.' He laughed and drank again. "Yes sir, Mr. Charles Thomas, I'm liable ta be in the dowg house fer these hyare, but I couldn't hardly stand throwin back all them purty crabs."

Charles Thomas watched the eggs and the guts drifting in the water. That's when he spotted the calm drifting forms of two big rock cruising over towards them just as slick as two thieves in the night. He could see their sharp, black stripes against their silver bodies, and he noted how the tips of the fins on their backs left a wake on the water's surface. They came up slow and lazy-like. Then, quick as lightning, they struck at the floating bits of crab, shaking their heads like dogs to break apart the sacks of eggs. Furry noticed them, too.

"Dast[31], Charles Thomas," he said with a chuckle, "whare's yer pole at now?"

Charles Thomas spat at one of the fish. The white glob struck the water and the closest fish eyed it but then swam on. Charles Thomas went back to staring at the crosses on the backs of Furry's arms, and he thought about why he'd come, working up his confidence. There was nothing he hated more than asking kid-ish questions – to his Uncle Furry more than anyone. But then, there was just something about this whole finding Jesus that for the life of him he couldn't square away in his head, like when you couldn't work out how figures went together. Here and now, standing before Furry, it seemed childish to have thought that his uncle was Jesus. It was more complicated than that.

Jesus was somehow both here and not here, like He had him an invisibility cloak or something. See, people talked to Him all the time, and that Visitin Preacher had

---

[31] Dast: An island euphemism for damn.

said He was here, so Jesus couldn't be dead. Yet of course He'd died and come back to life, and all that a good long time ago. So, in the end, how could you know if He was still alive or dead, or just what, or just where He could be found at either way. All day Charles Thomas and his Prayer Voice had thought He could be Furry, but now something about that didn't seem right. Suddenly figuring such things out seemed about the hardest thing there was. Furry was near done cleaning his lemons, and Charles Thomas knew his Uncle was liable to go for his nap soon as he was done, so, at last, Charles Thomas wrapped his knuckles on the dock again and said:

"Uncle Furry, if a man's got bidness with Jesus, how's he go 'bout fixin it up?"

His uncle's hands paused and the crosses stood at taut attention. He kept his shinning face down on the task before him and said, "Welp, me, I mostly pray on it whenever I'm got bidness with Lord Jesus. Read my Bible." Furry resumed pulling apart the crab in his hands. "And then sometime, when that don't feel like it's enough, I take'er to church to talk a piece."

"Yeah, but what if yer really just got to talk straight to Jesus?"

Furry broke from his work entirely, even though there were only two lemons left to be cleaned. He raised one stained white-rubber boot up and placed it on the warshboard[32], then he shucked off his gloves and reached his dead-white, pruney hand out to lay it on Charles Thomas's bare foot. The hand was cold and slimy as if over the years it had become one with the fish and crabs it worked. Furry kept those eyes on Charles Thomas's dirty feet and he said:

"Charles Thomas, the Lord's all the time listenin. Yer just got to Trust and Pray. That right thare's the meaning a' Faith."

Charles Thomas felt his Uncle didn't understand. Prayer and Faith were fine, but they didn't solve the question of whether you could find Jesus to talk to or not.

"But what if you need to see Him to talk to, you know face-to-face-like, so you can ask'im a thing er two."

Furry lifted his hand from Charles Thomas's foot and ran it through his shaggy hair. He squinted off across the water and the endless wilderness of marsh behind.

"I think I might got sumptin fer ye," he said after a long minute.

---

[32] Warshboard: The knee-high coping around the cockpit of a deadrise.

Furry headed up forward, stooping into the tiny cabin and was back again in no time. He had a pocket-sized, black leather Bible that was tattered as could be. He flipped towards the end through the crumbling, coffee-colored pages.

"This hyare was my Pap-pap's Bible. Yer Great Granpappy Abel's ol' King James Bible from aboard his skipjack[33] the *Henrietta P.*"

A handful of pages slipped out and Furry caught them before they hit the wet deck. Finally he stopped flipping. His finger ran the page and his lips moved within his beard. Then he fixed that bushy, red face of his on Charles Thomas and said, "Listen hyare; John fourteen, verses eighteen to thirty-one:

---

[33] Skipjack: The skipjack is America's last commercial fishing vessel working under sail. In the state of Maryland skipjacks are allowed to use large dredges to harvest oysters exclusively under sail in a law dating back to the 1870's. Skipjacks are shaped just like a deadrise workboat, but with a clipper bow. They are beamy and generally 40-50 feet long. A single aft-angled mast is placed far forward in the boat. A skipjack's boom is 2/3 the length of the mast, so long that the boom extends 4-6 feet past the stern. Skipjacks sail under a huge main and a jib. By law they are not allowed to have an engine aboard the boat so all skipjacks have a small pusher-boat that hangs in davits from the stern when sail dredging. When not dredging, the pusher-boat is tied to the stern to motor the skipjack where need be. Every cold month of the year a few skipjacks continue to harvest oysters from the Chesapeake as their countless predecessors have for well over 100 years. (Maryland laws have changed in recent years to allow for some power dredging making the continued existence of the skipjack fleet questionable).

"Jesus said, 'I will not leave ye comfortless: I will come to you.

"'Yet in a little while, and the world seeth me no more; but ye sees me: 'cause I live, ye shall live also.

"'At that day ye shall know that I'm in my Father, and ye in me, and I in you.

"'He that hath my commandments, and keepeth them, he it is that loveth me: and he that loveth me shall be loved of my Father, and I will love him, and will manifest myself to him.'

"Judas saith unto him, not Iscariot, 'Lord, how is it that thou wilt manifest thyself unto us, and not unto the world?'

"Jesus answered and said unto him, 'If a man love me, he'll keepth my Words: and my Father'll love him, and we'll come unto him, and make our home wit him.

"'He that loveth me not, keepeth not my sayins: and the Word which yer heardt is not mine, but the Father's which sent me.

"'These things have I spoken unto you, bein yet present witchee[34].

"'But the Comforter, which is the Holy Ghost, whom the Father'll send in my name, He shall teach ye all

---

[34] 'Witchee': Jtown for 'with you'

things, and bring all things to yer remembrance, whatsoever I'm said unto you.

"'Peace I leave witchee, my peace I give unto you: not as the world giveth, give I unto you. Let not yer heart be troubled, neither let it be afraid.

"'Yer heardt how I said unto you, I go away, and come again unto you. If ye loved me, ye'd rejoice, 'cause I said, I go unto the Father: fer my Father is greater'an I.

"'And now I'm tolt ye 'fore it come to pass, that, when it is come to pass, ye might believe.

"'Hereafter I'll not talk much witchee: fer the prince of this world cometh, and hath nothin in me. But that the world may know that I love the Father; and as the Father gave me Commandment, even so I do.

"'Arise, let us go hence.'"

When Furry finished he closed the book, carefully putting the loose pages back to rights, then he looked at Charles Thomas.

"D'ye understood a little better now?"

Charles Thomas was far more confused than he'd been when he'd found Furry, but his Uncle had such a satisfied look on his face that Charles Thomas nodded and said, "Sure 'nough, Uncle Furry, sure 'nough."

Furry closed one eye against the glare of the sun and squinted up at Charles Thomas like he was trying to guess his weight.

"See it's like The Book says, the Holy Spirit is God's Helper and the Holy Spirit's inye, and it's like a go-between 'tween you and Jesus, who's like a go-between 'tween Man and the Father-God? See now? Just like it says! And that's why yer got ta act right and Pray and have Faith. For it's with eyes of Faith that we see that Jesus is with us everywhere we go!"

Charles Thomas bobbed his head along like the old church ladies and said, "Mhmm, mmhmm, that's fair awright, deed that's fair." Furry grinned all over and went to put his Bible away.

The truth was it was all such a mixed up ball of words that Charles Thomas couldn't help but let his mind wander the whole time Furry'd been talking. He knew he kept hearing the word Father, and he figured Furry was talking about God and also maybe his Father, and maybe that was the key to it all. The word *love* come up a lot, too – more than Charles Thomas was accustomed to hearing. And he heard some part about making your home with your Father (could be important), but dern it was a confusing mess, and before he could figger it all out Furry came back and said,

"What ye say we make us a Loop er two on the bike?"

"That's fair," Charles Thomas said again.

Furry eyed the last two lemons to be cleaned in the bottom of the basket. Then he chuckled and said, "It's yer lucky day girls! Yer been saved!" as he up-ended the basket over the side. The two crabs seemed like they were swimming before they were wet, and in a second they'd disappeared into the shadows beneath The County Dock.

Furry hoisted up the basket of cleaned lemons and said, "Take this hyare will ye," before passing them up onto the dock. Then, he smacked his forehead theatrically and said, "Dast! I'm near fergot yer peelers." Furry gave a wink and then out of nowhere – like magic! – he produced a slimy plastic shopping bag. Charles Thomas could see the limp forms of three or four peelers inside the bag. Furry passed the bag up to Charles Thomas before leaping up on to the dock, nimble as a cat.

Furry carried his basket of lemons, and Charles Thomas carried his dripping sack of peelers. Furry's motorcycle was there at the end of Wilkens, enough off to the side that Charles Thomas hadn't noticed it on his way out the County Dock. Furry's bike had its strange, home-welded cart hitched behind. Furry set his basket in the cart among the jumble of oily tools and motor oil cans. Charles Thomas set his bag of peelers there, too. Furry straddled the bike and with one specific kick he brought the motor to life with a lovely roar. Charles Thomas climbed up behind Furry, getting that feeling he always got like he was king of the world astride his throne, and off they went with a rumble and a clatter.

Normally it was then, astride that growling motorcycle, that things became simple at last. Many an afternoon or evening Furry rode Charles Thomas around The Loop of the island, and it was like every ache and itch left him; there wasn't a skeeter or a greenhead[35] to worry him; the locusts were drowned out and his Prayer Voice was pleased. The heat departed and the breeze washed him clean. For once he didn't miss all the things he didn't have, as if – in some oasis – his spirit and his flesh had found peace at last.

But that afternoon peace wouldn't come, for the guilt of his sins followed at arm's length. Around every corner Rooster, or Miss Barb, or his Mom could be waiting.

[35] 'Greenhead': North American greenheaded fly (Tabanus nigrovittatus), a terrible biting fly that is prolific on the island.

Nowhere was safe from judgment, as if angels were circling above, seeing all and yet waiting to strike.

Furry drove The Loop, tracing the island's parameter, making the first left at Callahan's and heading south down East Water Street, along the island's Creekside, towards The Bridge. At the four-way stop by The Bridge, Furry crossed Main and pointed north so as to follow the Bayside up West Water Street. The breeze off the Bay made the flags snap and Charles Thomas's thin hair stand up. His heart climbed higher and higher in his throat the closer they got to Miss Barb and Mr. Bill Pinder's house on the corner of West Water and Sun Street.

Charles Thomas spotted Rooster's truck first, and then, to his horror, he saw Miss Barb in her yard. (Didn't she have anything better to do than spend her life in her front yard?!). Miss Barb caught sight of them too, and she straightened as they bent her corner. But just then, as luck would have it, Furry spotted a pretty woman walking halfway along Sun Street, and he got too distracted to see Miss Barb's flailing arms.

The pretty woman was Charles Thomas's friend RJ's mom. Furry gunned the engine towards her, then slowed a hair and hollered, "No, ye ain't no good,"[36] to which RJ's mom had just enough time to holler back, "Franklin, git on away from hyare an' home to yer wife!" before Furry accelerated and they turned south off of Sun Street and disappeared down the safety of Loblolly Lane.

Once on Loblolly they were again on the east side of the island, paralleling the dark, swirling Creek. Loblolly was tranquil and shady as always. Furry made the engine roar so a pair of marsh hens took flight, and people looked up from their porches and yards.

They finished The Loop by returning to Wilkens where they'd begun. As they neared Callahan's again, Charles Thomas spotted the group of swimmers he'd seen in The Creek earlier. They were all a few years older than him, and he looked up to them immensely. RJ, Boogie-3 and Mikey Jr. were shirtless, drinking Cokes and laughing at something. Lily was there too, like the queen of the parade, wearing a bikini top and khaki shorts that showed the wet lines of a bathing suit beneath. Furry mashed his horn, and they swaggered to the edge of the street with deliberate slowness. That was when Charles Thomas

---

[36] 'No, ye ain't no good.': 'You are good looking.' This is a common, flirtatious way for a Jtown man to compliment a woman's beauty. Despite the paramount importance of religion on the island, islanders tend to be quite flirty with each other.

spotted Dolores in their midst. For the second time in as many minutes alarm bells went off in his head. His pride shook like a leaf in a blow, thinking what Dolores might be telling them older kids.

Furry called out with a laugh, "Git on out the street, ye dernt delinquents!"

Charles Thomas kept his head down, not wanting to see RJ's arm as it stretched out mockingly. Despite the engine's rumble he could feel their laughter hotly climbing up in his head and making his ears turn red. Furry didn't notice a thing though, and in a second they had turned north onto Main Street and started up through the heart of town.

One block up Main, at the intersection with Market, the street was blocked by an odd-looking group headed southward towards them. A round, middle-aged woman named Rhonda Cator was pushing her ancient father in a wheelchair. Beside her was Rhonda's even-rounder daughter, Marg, who was pushing a baby carriage. This time Furry didn't mash on his horn. Instead he slowed to join the group.

Charles Thomas felt like he was being attacked from all directions: the fear of Miss Barb and Rooster to the north; the swimmers and their shame-laden laughter to the south; and here was God pinning him down, exposed in the middle of it all. Time to beg: *Please Jesus, please! I swear you save me from this an' I'll never cuss again. I'll pick up trash. I'll carry ol' church folks's groceries. I'll wear my W.W.J.D.? shirt to school on the first day back (You know I only don't wear it 'cause it's a hair small!). Please, Jesus. I'm prayin to ye now, you get me out a' this an' I swear I'll... I'll send all my allowance to a starving kid in Israel! I'm begging you please don't let 'em catch me here like this. Please, Lord, please!*

Furry cut the engine and the locusts swelled to fill the silence. Charles Thomas figgered he was screwed, glued and tattooed.

"What ye say thare, Rhonda; Marg; Cap'n Ward?" Furry called. Everyone nodded and said Hi except the old man who stared off indifferently. "Yer got the new baby out fer her first Loop, huh, Marg?"

Marg chewed on her gum and just nodded her head. It was Rhonda who beamed her horsey face at them and said with a sweep of her arm, "Furry, Charles Thomas, meet our newest little islander: Dinah Leah Cator-Pinder."

Furry put the kickstand down and got off the bike to have a look at what was wrapped up in the baby carriage. Charles Thomas reluctantly descended, too. He knew this was one of those things on the island, like dressing up for church, that you just had to do whether you liked it or not. The blacktop was plenty hot on his barefeet.

"Dern if she ain't a spittin image of ye Cap'n!" Furry chuckled.

Charles Thomas studied the old man, imagining what might be in the baby carriage. Scars and brown lumps dotted the old man's bald head. He was missing half an ear, and Charles Thomas could tell from how Captain Ward's wrinkled mouth curved inward that he didn't have a tooth-one. Everything about the old man seemed ruined by age, and yet his eyes shone outward as if they'd captured all the fire of a lifetime's suns.

"Dast," was all the old man said. He sucked in his lips and then blew out a wad of spit.

Rhonda caught Charles Thomas staring at the old man, and she said, all shiny-like, "Don't ye worry 'bout Daddy, Charles Thomas. Come on and meet lil Dinah!"

Charles Thomas saw that everybody – except Captain Ward – was watching him closely. He approached and rose to his toes to peer into the baby carriage. Wrapped up in a blanket was this bald, wrinkly, red thing that looked like a shriveled hotdog that had been cooked much too long in the microwave. He fell back a bit and blurted out, "Whatdaellzat?"

"A big, beautiful, baby girl: nine pound four ounces!" Rhonda crowed.

"And dern if she ain't got her momma's eyes," Furry said in a way that Charles Thomas knew was him finding something nice to say.

"Everbody says the same," Marg informed the group.

Charles Thomas was staring at Marg with his mouth drooping open, and then with a pinch of shame he caught them all watching him.

Rhonda spoke up: "What? Ain't ye knowed Marg was havin a baby, Charles Thomas?"

"I just figurt she was getting fat," he blurted out.

The old man erupted, laughing and coughing so hard Charles Thomas was afraid he might fall out his chair. Furry was laughing too, but trying to hold himself back.

"Stop it Daddy, stop it! That ain't a bit funny," Rhonda snapped. "If you cain't act civil I can take ye home."

"I ain't wanta be out hyare no how!" The old man said, sucking in his lips to spit again.

"Ain't you 'shamed? Actin that way when yer got a new great-grandbaby ta be celebratin?"

"Be Damned to ashes anyhow! Cain't none a' ye have a boy chilt?!"

Everyone was bickering, and it was all his fault, but it kinda pleased Charles Thomas in a way, like it was a sin his soul enjoyed. His Prayer Voice started asking what Jesus would think of all that. Charles Thomas reckoned he was pretty sinful, and then, just then, (like it was the hand of God striking down at him) Charles Thomas caught sight of the nose of Rooster's rusty truck turning south from Sun Street onto the northernmost part of Main, just two blocks away. Without a second's thought Charles Thomas felt the Devil in his legs again, and he took off into the backyards along Main, hopping fences – pain stabbing up his broke arm each time – just as quick and slick as a bleeding fish running from the hook in his cheek.

Charles Thomas felt the sure, hot fingers of judgment closing in around him as he ran. He couldn't be certain if Rooster had seen him at all, or if he was giving chase or not, but in Charles Thomas's mind every bush and branch felt like Rooster's gnarled hands snatching at his clothes. The beat of his own heart rang out like footsteps on his trail. He darted and dashed along, avoiding streets and ducking in the cover of houses and hedges until he came out into the shady, narrow alleyway between The New Believers Church and the Parsonage.

The alleyway was damp and cool and protected from the street, and Charles Thomas knew the church was empty and locked at this hour on a Monday. He was safe – for the moment least.

He stood there panting with his hands on his knees and his arm pounding. Trickling lines of sweat were running down inside the cast, and he longed to be rid of the evil, painful, itchy thing. His Prayer Voice told him God was angry, and it all was bad to worse now. Rooster would tell Furry and Rhonda and everybody would know. The noose would tighten: judgment was at hand, and that meant Jesus wouldn't ever help him, and his arm was broke forever, and his Father was gone as yesterday. Good Lord, why were sins so easy and guilt so heavy?

Charles Thomas picked up a stick and shoved it down into his cast and dug around in there, scratching where it itched and hurt so he didn't have to think about anything else. And yet, then when he pulled the stick back out, dern if it didn't itch and hurt worse than ever. And now it burned like he'd cut it all up. *Christ, if there weretn't nare a fair turn in this whole life*, he thought. But then that Voice came back at him saying, *Dast if it ain't just what you deserve.* He sat down and leaned his head against the cool cinderblock foundation of The New Believer's Church. He closed his eyes and tried to find his flame again, to open his heart and ignore the feeling like his cast was full of fire ants, and that feeling like God was damning him for his sins and like the world was collapsing in on him.

And that's when Charles Thomas heard a very peculiar sound coming from the New Believers' Guest Parsonage. As usual, life's newest mystery diminished its last defeat, and Charles Thomas got up and went towards the source of the sound.

It sounded like someone was running on a treadmill and panting and groaning some, but then it also sounded like some girl had hurt herself and was quietly moaning in pain. The noises got louder as he approached an open window on the ground floor of the Parsonage. The window was too high to see in, so Charles Thomas drug over two cinderblocks, stacking them one on top of the other, and then he climbed up his wobbly tower to peer through the window screen.

There on a shadowy bed he could make out two bodies just as naked as Adam and Eve moving around like they were wrestling. First Charles Thomas recognized the long hair, beard and surprisingly tattooed body of the Visitin Preacher, and then, under the Visitin Preacher, he recognized the pimply face of a high-school-age island girl named Remi who helped lead the New Believers' Youth Prayer Group. It looked like the Visitin Preacher was trying to get something that he'd lost out from underneath of Remi. His hands were under her and the two of them were wriggling around like they were stuck. Remi's eyes were pinched shut and her pimple-pocked face was half hidden by her hair and pointed towards Charles Thomas and the open window. Her mouth was partially open, and she was making these little wounded noises so Charles Thomas couldn't tell if she was having fun or if the Visitin Preacher was hurting her. Then both of her hands seized the Visitin Preacher's white backside and each time he tried to pull away she yanked him back down on top of her – and then, without warning, the Visitin Preacher went as stiff as a fish when you chunk it against the dock, and he melted down on top of Remi. She patted his backside with one hand and murmured something, and then she brushed away her hair and locked eyes with Charles Thomas. Next thing she was screaming and tearing at the sheet to cover their nakedness, but the Visitin Preacher had already reeled around and caught sight of Charles Thomas, and he started screaming

"Jesus Christ! You little Fuck! You little Fuckin Pervert! I'll Fuckin teach you to peep in Fuckin windows!"

Charles Thomas's tower of cinderblocks toppled. He fell and felt his backside soaking up water from the damp mud. The Visitin Preacher busted through the window-screen and came flailing halfway out the window to try and catch hold of Charles Thomas. Charles Thomas rolled away just in time and took off out the shady alleyway.

He burst out into the sunny street like a wild-eyed horse galloping down Main Street without a thought but escape, and there, at the corner of Wilkens, he wrecked into the group of swimmers who were just turning up Main.

"Whoa, whoa, whoa, thare Trooper! Whare's the fahr[37]?" RJ yodeled.

Charles Thomas felt as if that fiery sword was splitting his head, like the angels of judgment were swarming like skeeters, like the trumpets of the Final Judgment were blasting. He stared behind him – eyes rolling, face dripping – and was shocked to see Main Street empty of persecutors.

"Dern if you ain't poor!" Mikey Jr. laughed.

[37] 'Fahr' = 'fire' (A classic Eastern Shore joke asks: "Why did the three wise men have ash on their feet? 'Cause they come from a fahr!")

"He's done sumptin," Lily said, "He's on the run is what he is."

Boogie-3 guffawed in his slack jaw way.

"It's that Visitin Preacher," Charles Thomas told them all, "He's after me!"

"Ain't nobody after you. Why'd he be after you?"

"'Cause I'm seent him and Remi wrastlin neckid! That's why!"

There was a pause, and then the group broke out cackling like crows.

"Damn if Trooper ain't seent nothing," RJ said appreciatively.

"Dast, Mariah sure 'nough did say she seent Remi and that preacher up to the Marshy Creek bridges!" Lily said, "But I ain't *never* thought she'd let him get all that far after no more'an a weekend. Christ Alive!"

"Gawddamn if Trooper ain't seent nothing," RJ repeated, slapping Charles Thomas on the back.

Charles Thomas felt a swelling pride. He didn't fully understand, but he knew he'd witnessed something important, and he wanted to expand his influence.

"Don't know what they was wrastlin over," he reported, "but I think she won 'cause he quit first."

Again the group hooted, and this time RJ's arm came up pointing in Charles Thomas's face.

"You dummy! They wasn't wrastlin. They was sleepin together."

Charles Thomas wasn't gonna be made a fool this time he knew what he'd seen. "Nuh-uh; no, no RJ. They weretn't sleepin none."

Lily doubled over, covering her face like she was embarrassed by just how funny all this was. The boys were all laughing at him like he was dumber than a hardhead[38].

"Sex, Dumbass, Sex! They was doing Sex, ye Retard."

Charles Thomas was dumbfounded.

Mikey Jr. was saying, "I knowed that preacher was a fake since I set eyes on him. You could spot that fake accent from a mile off. Pop-pop says the feller's from New Jersey er some Shit like that. Says he just does all this preachin fer money."

"That weretn't what you was sayin after Sunday Service," RJ said. "You said he was cool. Dast if I don't remember!"

---

[38] 'Hardhead': The Atlantic Croaker, or 'hardhead' as it's known in the Chesapeake, is a fish famous for its gullibility with any bait and its stubborn reluctance to die, thus the moniker.

The group broke down into bickering. Charles Thomas felt dizzy – his head swum in the sun, his throat was dry as sand; it was like he couldn't tell up from down. The Visitin Preacher was a fake? Remi and him were doing Sex, that giant sin that everybody was always warning them against. And the Visitin Preacher was from New Jersey: he was a fake? And then an Evil Voice came to him saying, *And if all that was fake, then what else was fake? Ye knowed all along ain't ye? And so, what about you an' findin Jesus, ye idiot? Ye Gawddamned Retarded toadfish.*

The group suddenly came to some truce, and the bickering ceased before Charles Thomas had time enough to sort out this newest nuclear explosion of doubt.

RJ's cracking voice crowed, "I'm near fergot to tell ye, Charles Thomas: we're all seent Dolores up to The Store." Charles Thomas's heart pitched over a very specific precipice. The group started giggling, and then RJ dropped the punch line.

"She says yer out lookin fer Jesus ta fix yer arm!"

The group broke down again, every one of them laughing in his face like they knew everything.

"Lil Charles Thomikins is lookin fer Jesus! Gawddamn, I thought you couldn't get no dummer'an jumpin off a ruff ... but Christ if ye ain't found somehow to be dumber still!"

Their laughter climbed into Charles Thomas's head beside the throb of the locusts. The din grew unbearable so he couldn't even think nor make sense of nothing.

"Hey Thomikins," RJ hollered when he caught his breath, "when you find Jesus can ye ask'im whare Santy Claus is at?"

"And the Easter Bunny!"

Charles Thomas felt, with an urgent certainty, that first and foremost his pride had been damaged all but beyond repair. Shame and anger stabbed about murderously within his mind, body and soul. Suddenly his hatred for Dolores, and all the embarrassment and doubt she'd given him swelled and swelled, obliterating his inner light like an eclipse. He knew there was but one solution for this: he had to fix her for all she'd done. And it had to be public and it had to be now.

"Which way'd Dolores go at?" Charles Thomas called out into them older kids' laughs.

"Back on north up Main, towards her mum-mum's place."

"Come on," Charles Thomas said cool as he could, "I'ma show ye what I think a' Dolores and all her lies."

He said it just as strong and convincing as he could muster, and then he turned on his heel and pointed himself northward towards Dolores's mum-mum's house up on Cross Street.

"So yer sayin she's lyin?" RJ called after him, "She's makin it all up?"

"Yeah right, Charles Thomas! Why in the Devil'd she wanta do all that?"

Charles Thomas didn't bother to give an answer because he knew he didn't have one; he just kept marching north up Main. He felt a relieving wave of pride and strength break over him then, for he heard the older kids jogging to catch up. He tried to focus on just what he was going to do when he stood before Dolores, but his mind ran from that thought to stumble about in this new wilderness of doubt.

The Visitin Preacher was a fake, and they talked like there was no more a Jesus Christ than there was a Santy Claus! So, did that mean it was all fake? Even the power and the fire of the Spirit that he'd felt burning all this time? And Jesus being on the island and doing like you asked, like the Visitin Preacher and his Prayer Voice had said?

As that thought passed through his mind Charles Thomas heard a cruel laughter begin to build within his head. It started as a low rumble like that of distant drums, and it swelled like the evil locusts, wiping out every thought and sound. And then, suddenly, it cut off. Charles Thomas felt an immediate, empty hollowness invade his soul. He searched desperately for that torch of a flame, but its light and warmth were gone, leaving only the nothingness of loss that he couldn't help but probe like the gap of a lost tooth. He nearly stopped dead in the street with the shock of it all, but then behind him he heard the older kids joking and jeering about what he was liable to do. In another wave, his strength and rage returned, and he thought: this was all Dolores's fault, this doubt, this shame, this pain and loss. It was all her fault – like it was all his Mom's fault he didn't have a Father – and now Dolores was gonna pay. Charles Thomas felt a rage flooding through his arms and his fingertips, and he heard that Voice saying: *That Dolores, she's gonna pay dearly now.*

Dolores was there, in her mum-mum's sideyard on Cross St. She was crouched by a spigot, making mud pies by herself. At the sight of her fragile, sad little form in that blue dress, hunched over alone in the mud, Charles Thomas felt his wrath become fear. But then he heard the group whispering behind his back, and RJ called, "Charles Thomas ain't gonna do Shit, 'cause it's all true anyhow."

The time had come for Charles Thomas to act. There was nothing else to do. He couldn't run this time. He bent and picked up a stone from the gravel patch where Dolores's mum-mum parked her truck, and he shouted, "Dolores Pinder, I'ma teach you ta tell lies on me!"

The movement of his arm throwing the first stone took a surprising amount effort, as if the air had turned thick as water. Charles Thomas's stone fell short of Dolores, but then a rock came humming over Charles Thomas's head, striking Dolores in the side. She let out a little cry, and suddenly the air was filled with flying rocks, and then Charles Thomas couldn't tell the difference between his rocks and the others. Dolores ran, stones swarming her like a plague, and Charles Thomas and his mob gave chase around the house where Dolores disappeared into the back door before they could inflict yet more damage still.

For a moment everything was silent except the locusts – they continued their chant unchanged. Charles Thomas felt like he had been dropped from a great height and had landed on his feet with a jolt. The air seemed to have a smoky, painted quality, as if they were suspended in the silence after battle. The mob hung like laundry, all surprised by the sudden departure of spirit. It was Dolores, inside the house, who broke the silence with a soul-piercing wail. Then a disembodied voice of womanly power called out from the darkness within:

"Names! I want names!"

Dolores's mum-mum smashed through the screen door like a chimney falling down upon the children. They scattered in all directions with that voice rumbling after them: "I know ye! I know all a'ye! Justice will be had. If it won't be served by yer wicked parents it will be done on that Final Day! You-all will stand Judgment, and Justice will be had!"

Charles Thomas felt the old panic of sin take hold as they all ran, but then he heard the older kids laughing just as free as birds. A new power filled his emptiness, and he pushed away the idea of sins and judgments like he was leaving his old skin behind. He followed RJ until they broke out into the blaring sun of Sun Street. RJ ran on towards People's Park, but that was where Charles Thomas was struck frozen stiff, for there, at the end of Sun Street by the park, was the mailman Mr. Bill Pinder talking to his wife Miss Barb at their front gate. Sins or not, earthly consequences were still at hand.

Mr. Bill and Miss Barb looked up as RJ passed their gate at a sprint. Before Charles Thomas could know for sure whether they'd seen him or not he turned and ran for the closest refuge available: the backyards of the black houses along Sun Street where he figured they might just let him be. He ran, painfully hopping fences, until he spotted a big chinaberry bush that made a fortress close to the ground, and, after glancing around to confirm he was alone, Charles Thomas rolled under it to hide.

It was dark and smelled nice in the cool dirt under the chinaberry bush. For a little while the ground beneath him seemed to be moving, making him sick like he was out on the water in a gale. But, as his panting and his pounding heart slowed, things got better, and he got to feeling safe and alright beneath his bush.

He was definitely getting a whupping now: that thought came in a bitter flash. He figured he well enough deserved it, too, when he thought about little Dolores all alone making mud pies without a clue of what was coming. But then that old Prayer Voice spoke up, saying, *It ain't all yer fault. There were them others, too, and RJ's mom ain't gonna whup RJ none.* And then he thought he might just could get away with it too, if Dolores's mum-mum hadn't seen him. And maybe if Dolores kept her big mouth shut.

Fat chance thare! The Voice laughed right in his face, and with that familiar panic he felt his sins come rushing back, towering high up above him.

His stomach let out an angry growl, and Charles Thomas became acutely aware of his hunger and his thirst. He remembered he hadn't eaten or drunk a thing since breakfast. At once he felt a profound weakness and exhaustion take hold.

In other times he might have prayed. He might have repented hard as he could, what with such a tower of sin like what he'd built up in just one day. But there, in the shadowy dirt, after everything that had happened, he just couldn't bring himself to do it. He heard the older kids laughing in his face clear as if they were all around him now. They were laughing at him for looking for Jesus, saying there was no more Savior to be found than there was a Santy Claus. No more Jesus Christ than there was an Easter Bunny. It was a terrifying thought, to take what had always been and dump it out like that. That Voice with its new Evil tone started interrogating: *And what if there ain't no Christ – just like that Visitin Preacher weretn't nothing but a lie and a fake? What is, if sins don't mean nothin, so long as you can get away with 'em? What if there ain't no Jesus, no God, no Heaven, no Hell? What is, if sins ain't nothin but some story old folks tell to little kids to make 'em act right?'* Charles Thomas had never in his life thought such thoughts, and a storm of fear and self-loathing came lashing back at him harder than any whupping he ever got.

His mind rolled and writhed about in crossing waves. Everyone believed. Near everybody he knew, and he couldn't imagine any of them – his Mom, his Uncle Furry and his Aunt Sally, Reverend A.D. and his Sunday School teacher Miss Maggie, nearly every soul he'd ever known – without Church and Christ and God. In his own life Church had always been there, along with total confidence in Jesus and God. There was never a week without Sunday School, Wednesday night Bible study, church suppers, and chatting about the Bible with his Mom or his uncle or his teachers at school or anybody else. And then that Voice started saying, *If there ain't no Christ, nor sins, then thare ain't no soul, nor Heaven. And ye know then thare ain't no place for yer Father to be at.*

It was too much. Charles Thomas clutched his knees to his chest and rocked and rocked until it all went away. Gradually he came to some exhausted peace: maybe them older kids didn't know it all, or had been pullin his leg, or actin foolish?

But how could you know? Lord, he hated being a little kid and not knowing a thing. His stomach rumbled again. For a godless moment he imagined what the world would be like without Jesus and Christians. He saw crabs and locusts covering everything. Saw people walking on all fours, covered in fur, communicating in barks, burps and farts. People doing like the Visitin Preacher and Remi: doing Sex, All The Time! And if there wasn't any God, then the water would come flooding up with nothing to stop it, flooding up over everything, and all them parts of the world that weretn't water already surely would be. Then exhaustion mixed with fantasy, and the two together drug him slowly down into sleep.

In his vague dreams Charles Thomas had the feeling that shadowy figures were moving all around him, like angels and demons were stalking his soul. And then he woke up with a start to see Rodney towering into the chinaberry bush and blocking out the sun, his hands hanging from his wrists like bricks, his tangle of plastic gold chains and beads dangling from his neck, and his Oscar the Grouch sunglasses all twisted up in his hair and beard.

"Charlstoms's sleepin in a tree. Sleepin in a tree. I 'on't know why Charlstoms's sleepin in tree. Ha'h, ha'h, how come you sleepin in a tree Charlstoms?"

Charles Thomas didn't bother to reply (his Mom had told him he ain't need to worry 'bout things that Rodney said). But, after he got over his shock, he was happy Rodney'd found him, and he crawled out from under the bush and brushed himself off. Rodney was a relief. Ol' Rod was a favorite of the kids on the island because even though he was big as any man on the island Rodney never grew up, and that meant he was always good for a laugh. The afternoon sun was near unbearable, and so Charles Thomas went over and sat on the back step of Rodney's parents' house to hide from the sun in a small triangle of shade. Rodney followed Charles Thomas to the back step, but Rod didn't make any move to sit in the shade, or even step out of the brutal sun into what little shade could be had; no, he just stood there swaying in place and grinning down at Charles Thomas with those teeth of his that looked like a child's because they were so tiny and far apart.

"What you got that on yer arm fer, Charlstoms? You hurt yerself, Charlstoms?"

"Yeuh, I'm broke this hyare arm testin a parachute, you know what I mean?"

"You fall down an' got hurt, Charlstoms?"

"Sumptin like 'at."

"Why you do that, Charlstoms?"

"Well I ain't do it on purposed."

"I 'ont know why you do that," Rodney said shaking his head. "'Zit hurt, Charlstoms?"

"Yeuh it hurt awright, but I ain't never cried a bit."

"Charlstoms hurt hisself. Why you do that, Charlstoms?"

"Don't worry 'bout it, Rodney. It ain't nothin."

"I on't know why you do that, Charlstoms."

Rodney looked as though he was concerned about Charles Thomas's mental-wellbeing, as if Charles Thomas was the crazy one! He leaned in close like he wanted to touch the broken arm. Charles Thomas's first instinct was to get away, but then, he had the realization that if there was one person on this whole island that would hear him out for trying to find Jesus without making fun of him, it was Rodney. (Charles Thomas knew Rodney's family never missed a service at Bethel AME, the island's little black church, so he figured Rodney could understand somewhat.)

He studied Rodney's face for a moment, taking in the knotted, kinky hair on his chin and head, and the way Rodney's tongue moved all around like it wanted to escape.

He heard RJ in his head saying, *Rodney ain't nothin but a idiot baby! Dern if he don't cry all the time over nothing, even old as he is. Shoot, Rod, he won't never be a man, dern big, dumb baby.* Then he remembered what Miss Maggie said about how, *The Lord loves them that's special most of all,* and then Charles Thomas started telling the story of his day.

When he first told Rodney that he'd been looking for Jesus to fix his arm and to bring back his Father, Rodney looked cross, like he thought Charles Thomas might be playing a trick on him. But then, when Charles Thomas told him all about what the Visitin Preacher had said, Rodney started swaying like a tree in a storm, calling out, "Charlstoms gonna find Jesus. Charlstoms gonna find Jesus."

Charles Thomas told Rodney about what had happened with Rooster, and how it had seemed like Rooster was The One. How his arm was good as fixed – up 'til the paint messed it up. But then he told Rod about how Rooster probably couldn't be Jesus anyhow because of all the Evil things Rooster'd cussed him with, and how Rooster'd chased after him.

That was when Rodney started pacing around the little fenced in yard with his arms pumping up and down like he was trying to fly, saying, "Oooowee, ooowee Charlstoms in trouble. Ooowee oooweee Charlstoms in trouble."

Then he told Rodney about finding Dolores in the graveyard, and her laughing at him, and about Calhoon and Marsha and the tourists. And all what Marsha had said about talking to Jesus. He told Rodney about Furry, and what Furry had read to him about finding the Father, and then all about their Loop, and spotting the swimmers talking to Dolores, and then about the Cator family and how old Captain Ward had laughed when Charles Thomas had said what he said about Marg being fat.

Then, when Charles Thomas got to the part about the Parsonage, and the sounds, and what all he'd seen through the window, Rodney got so excited that he started pulling at his ears with one hand and sucking on the fingers of the other as he high-stepped around the yard. Charles Thomas liked the effect this part was having on Rodney. It fully dawned on him just how much he'd seen, and he went on elaborating on little details to make Rodney squeal. But then, just before Charles Thomas was gonna tell Rodney about what Remi's hands had done on the Visitin Preacher's backside, and how the Visitin Preacher had gone stiff all over, a deep commanding voice, mere inches from Charles Thomas's back scared the Devil right out of him.

"You can stop right thare, Charles Thomas," the voice said, "Cain't you see yer getting ol' Rod all worked up fer nothin?"

Mr. Abe Johnson, Rodney's dad, the town librarian and the only island accountant, was standing behind the screen door like a scarecrow, watching over the scene in his backyard. He was a skinny man – so skinny you could see the bones beneath the skin. He had a pair of round, metal glasses, a beard that traced his jaw, and a slate-grey vest over his stiff white shirt.

"Sound's like yer had quite the morning thare, Charles Thomas. How 'bout you take a little break and come in the parlor to have a glass a' lemonade with me an' Rod?"

Before Charles Thomas could figure out how to say no, Rodney bounded over in three earthshaking steps and snatched up his hand, pulling Charles Thomas to his feet and dragging him into the house.

It was darker and cooler inside. Rodney drug Charles Thomas into the living room where Mr. Abe calmly and caringly separated the two, telling Rodney to sit on the couch and work on his magazines. Rodney sat like a falling mountain, picked up a pen and opened a magazine from a scattered pile on the coffee table. He circled a few words and pictures before giving up to stare at Charles Thomas with his mouth partway open.

Charles Thomas tried his best to ignore Rodney's stare. Mr. Abe had disappeared into the kitchen. Charles Thomas felt like he was suddenly stranded in a foreign land. The first thing that appeared in the boy's mind came out his mouth: "I'm never been in no black house afore."

"Welp, thare's a first time fer everthing, Charles Thomas," Mr. Abe called back from the kitchen.

Charles Thomas didn't know what else to say, and so he busied himself with taking in his peculiar new surroundings. The living room was overflowing with thousands of antique-looking knickknacks and stuff. Nearly every square inch of wall was covered in bookshelves, densely packed glass cases, and framed pictures of boats and people and maps of Johnsontown and the like. There were all these ancient photos of black folks in the picking houses, or on workboats, old black ladies in long dresses and bonnets in front of a tiny church, barefoot black children grouped together in front of a school in the marsh. There was a wood-rimmed dip net and ice hooks and a glass washboard and neat, old handcarved boat models and decoys mounted all around. It was too much for Charles Thomas's eyes to take in.

"Do all black people's houses have so much stuff in 'em, Mr. Abe?"

Mr. Abe laughed in the kitchen. Rodney copied with a very exaggerated convulsion of his own that stopped as abruptly as it began.

"No," Mr. Abe called, "We're a bit diffrnt in this family. I'm what you might call a amateur historian. Either that, er a pack rat, dependin on whuther ye ask me er my wife."

"But, I mean, what ye got all this stuff for?"

Mr. Abe reentered the living room carrying three empty glasses and an iced pitcher of lemonade on a tray. Rodney started rocking and pulling at his plastic chains when he saw the lemonade. Charles Thomas eyed the dripping pitcher too and was instantly hollowed out by thirst. Mr. Abe paused in front of a really old map of Johnsontown, back when the island was three times the size and all different shaped.

"You know, Charles Thomas, one day this whole island of ours is gonna be gone beneath the wuter. I'm spent my whole life – since I was a boy like you – collectin old island artifacts and junk. That an' writin a bit of a history so there'll be a record for the days when it's all gone."

"Uncle Furry told me all that's bird crap, 'bout the island disappearin. Uncle Furry says all we need's more of a jetty, and that'll stop the 'rrosion," Charles Thomas informed Mr. Abe.

Mr. Abe looked at him sadly and said, "That jetty might could stop the erosion, but it cain't stop them rising seas."

"Yeuh, but Uncle Furry says all that's bird crap anyhow, and we ain't goin nowheres."

Mr. Abe set the tall glasses on the coffee table and said, "Welp, maybe it's best to see it that way. Let the sleepin dowg sleep on. I'm sure I don't know." Mr. Abe shook his head. "But fer now, how 'bout sumptin we can all agree on: how 'bout a glass a' cold lemonade for a hot summer's day?"

Mr. Abe started pouring three glasses without waiting for Charles Thomas's response. Rodney grabbed the first full glass and drained it in ten seconds flat.

Charles Thomas's stomach rumbled once again, and he was so thirsty he felt like his tongue was shriveling up. But even feeling like that he couldn't be sure just what his Mom or Furry would say about drinking black people's lemonade. He knew well enough there were certain lines you didn't cross, like Calhoon's story about Cann and Dookie's wife, Miss Jude. You just couldn't ever tell how people on the island would act when it came to the lines between black and white. Not to mention the whole thing with Black Magic! He imagined drinking the lemonade and heading home only to find out it had turned him black as Dino mud. His Mom freaking out. Trying to chase him out the house with a broom like she had that one time a possum got in the house. Then him convincing her: *Mom, it's me Charles Thomas Parks. I swear. My favorite food is crab cobbler and icebox cake, and I have a scar on my wrist from when I fell through the coffee table.* Then she'd believe him, and she'd march right up there to Mr. Abe's and demand for him to turn Charles Thomas white again. A dernt fiasco is what that would be!

Finally, having resolved himself to take a strong, manly moral stance, Charles Thomas said, "Thanks, but no Mr. Abe. See I'm got a real busy day."

Mr. Abe left Charles Thomas's glass sweating on the coffee table and took up his own. He sipped it quietly, standing and watching Charles Thomas the whole time. Then he said, "Whole island's talkin 'bout how busy a day yer had already, Charles Thomas. How 'bout you just relax here an' chat with me an' Rod for a bit." He paused. Charles Thomas didn't make a move for the glass nor the nearest chair. Then Mr. Abe said, "You might's well sit down a hair. I'm already called yer Mom down at Skipjacks. She's gonna be comin up soon as she's done her shift."

Charles Thomas felt trapped and betrayed. Sure 'nough, it was just like some old timer had said to Furry that one time: you couldn't trust 'em no further than you could chunk a pile of bricks! (Which had confused Charles Thomas at the time because how were trust and distance related? And were you throwing one brick at a time or trying to chunk the whole pile at once? And who was 'them'? But now Charles Thomas knew 'them' was Black Mr. Abe. Black Mr. Abe who had just stabbed Charles Thomas in the back.). Charles Thomas considered various options of fleeing, finding all but the window blocked. Mr. Abe was standing firmly between him and any door to anywhere.

"Have a seat, Charles Thomas. I think I'm got something you might like to see."

Charles Thomas grudgingly took a seat in a chair across from Rodney and watched the lemonade sweat, proud of his strong, manly moral stance. Mr. Abe went to the bookshelves and selected a handful of old Jtown Elementary School yearbooks.

"Lemme see here now," Mr. Abe was saying to himself as he flipped through the books, "'92 or '93… Ah yeuh, thare he is: kindergarten 1993." He brought the book over and held it up in front of Charles Thomas. "You know who this here is?"

Charles Thomas looked. Mr. Abe's long finger was pointing to a photo of a sullen looking boy with a jagged haircut. For a second, Charles Thomas thought it was a picture of himself. Then Mr. Abe pulled back his finger revealing the name: Joseph Parks.

"You don't favor him none,"[39] Mr. Abe said, watching Charles Thomas closely.

Charles Thomas took the book into his hands and peered into the face of his Father as a child.

"I'm heard all what you were tellin Rod out back, and what with Father's Day yesterdee and all, I sorta put two and two together," Mr. Abe was saying. Charles Thomas stared and stared at the little face, only hearing the sounds of what Mr. Abe was saying like the words were waves on a distant beach. Despite the coolness of the shadowy living room he felt like his head was being cooked

[39] Jtown backspeak: "You look just like him."

in the sun, and his vision seemed to be swirling like water down a drain. All he could see was the picture of the sullen little boy with his tan skin, his thin hair, and his mouth half open like he was about to cuss you. Mr. Abe was flipping through more yearbooks and spreading them out before Charles Thomas on the coffee table.

"Here he was in second grade like you was last year. And here he was dressed up like Steve Urkel for Halloween. That I most certainly do remember," Mr. Abe said. "And then here's him as a fifth grader playing Joseph in the Christmas pageant."

In some of the pictures he was smiling or posing with friends. In others he was looking wicked like he'd just played a prank on you. But in all the pictures there was something cutting about that mirror image that Charles Thomas couldn't understand, that he couldn't get his mind around: how could this be the face of the Father of a son, the face of a man that had disappeared and not come back and so must have died? How could that little boy – so like Charles Thomas – do all that? It all hit him so hard, and with no warning at all, that Charles Thomas couldn't understand a thing, but he could feel a rage rising in his throat and chest, and then spreading to his hands and arms, right down to his fingertips. It made him just want to tear it all up into pieces and stomp on it and then burn it all up.

"I think I might have some more pictures from when he was a teenager here in one of these photo albums from the early 2000's," Mr. Abe was saying as he headed back to the bookshelf.

Charles Thomas looked up from the book in his hands and found that Mr. Abe had turned all cloudy and starry like he was trapped in a kaleidoscope.

Rodney spotted it first.

"Why Charlstoms cryin? I on't know why Charlstoms is cryin."

Charles Thomas felt the rage and shame crashing around within him, and he wanted to scream: *Stop it! Stop it now!* but he was being strangled, and he couldn't breath and words wouldn't come.

"It's alright to feel sad, Charles Thomas. I know you miss not having him around. Go ahead an' take a minute if ye need to. Me an' Rod can give ye some space." Mr. Abe left his place in the doorway and moved over towards his son on the couch so as to shepherd Rodney from the room.

The idea that they – Rodney and Mr. Abe – were both trying to make him cry flooded over Charles Thomas like a hurricane tide, and he fought it, and he fought to find the meanest, nastiest thing he could think to say, and then he screamed it at the top of his lungs so that it came screeching out like bad brakes:

"Stop it you Niggers! Stop it now! Niggers! Niggers! Niggers!"

Mr. Abe froze with his long delicate fingers on his giant child's arm. He fixed his whole, boney face on the little boy before him, looking for all the world like Charles Thomas had just smashed something he loved dearly. Rodney's face looked concerned, same as when he'd spotted Charles Thomas's broken arm, and he started asking, "Why you hollerin, Charlstoms; why you hollerin?" though no one was paying Rod any mind.

Mr. Abe kept that long, hard-jawed face fixed on Charles Thomas, and then he said, slow and heavy as if each word were a stone, "Charles Thomas, you don't know what yer sayin child; but Lord I'm sorry you know it a-tall."

"I know what Nigger means! It means yer black and dumb and mean," Charles Thomas bellowed at Mr. Abe just as loud as he could. He knew tears were streaking his face, but the yelling at least made him feel in control of his own throat once again.

"No," Mr. Abe replied, so quiet he was almost whispering, "Mostly it says more about the person sayin it than the one they're sayin it to."

Charles Thomas felt he had lost all control, like the Devil had swallowed him whole. His eyes fell on his un-drunk glass of lemonade, and his rage moved him like a kite in a storm: his hand grabbed the glass and dumped it all over the grinning pictures of his Father – Rodney screaming in shock – and then his arm reached back and chunked that glass as hard as he could at a glass-fronted display-case mounted to the wall before him. These were actions that moved at a different rate of time and space, nightmare-like, dense and crushing. He watched the solid wall of glass become a million falling slivers, as if the substance of the world had been irrevocably smashed.

Rodney screamed again and started crying. Mr. Abe was too shocked to move. And Charles Thomas? He ran, for in a world without sins it was all he could do. He ran through the shadowy house and out the back door. By the time the sun hit him he was blind from the tears and from the numbing shock of it all, but he ran on anyhow, breaking out into Sun Street and being stabbed and slashed by the shame of sobbing in the street. He felt as if the whole island was watching him and that they all hated him and were after him. And so he turned and ran for the only place on the island where he was sure there wouldn't be a soul: out into the bug-plagued marsh, out towards the end of Marshy Creek Road where the town brush pile waited to be burned like some monumental, out-of-place haystack jutting up from the marsh.

The road – half a mile of gravel, broken asphalt and oyster shells – cut his bare feet and turned his ankles as he pounded through the eternal puddles that tide left behind. Even as he ran the skeeters and the greenheads caught the scent of his soft, exposed skin. They swarmed his head and latched on to his moving limbs. Charles Thomas ran and ran – his chest feeling like a hole had opened up and he was being pierced clean through – across the two creosote bridges, all the way to where the road ran out. And at last, there before him stood the mountain of brush like a giant pagan idol waiting to be burned.

The greenheads and skeeters formed a black, buzzing cloud around his head and ankles the second that he stopped. He frantically beat the air with his good arm and his bad, screaming at the impotence of his effort and his pain, at the torture that was crawling over every inch of his skin. He howled as loud as he wanted because at last he was far enough away from the ever-watching eyes of town, alone where not a soul could see him. He cried like he had never cried in all his life. He sobbed and sobbed because he was broken, and it was all too much. Because his Father had been a little boy just like him, and he was as good as dead now and for forever after all the mess Charles Thomas had made. He cried because his Voice told him he'd committed the worst sin of his life, and he didn't want to hear that Voice or any other. That Voice was telling him he was a lemonade-throwin, rock-chunkin, paint-dumpin sinner of the worst kind, and Jesus wouldn't want him, and he'd be Damned straight to Hell. It told him that because of his badness his Father would never come back, and he was stuck with this awful, throbbing broke arm. It all gave him that feeling like he needed to run for the rest of his life, and he still wouldn't ever get away. His face streamed tears and snot and sweat. Patches of blood and welts covered his soft, hairless skin, and still the bugs wouldn't relent, nor would that feeling like Damnation was at hand.

A big greenhead bit him right between the eyes.

"Gawddamnit," he screamed into the emptiness. Then, "ShitCrap. Jesus Christ and Shit on it all. FuckBitch! TurdFart! GayCrap, PussyHeaded NiggerFart, Shit!" He screamed every sinful word he could think of, because at last he didn't care. He didn't want to care. Jesus weretn't real, and he ain't want Him no more nohow! All this about sins and Hell, well ShitCrap on that. All them people he knew, and church and everything. It was just a crop a PussyShit. They were all gonna hate him for what he done, so he'd just hate them right back. He felt a world crumbling within: it was like each new cuss word was another bomb falling on some city in his soul.

The boy stood there sobbing for a long time like he'd been nailed to the spot, but at last the bugs got so bad that he couldn't stand them a second longer. He knew he couldn't return to town now, or maybe ever. The nearest thing to protection he had out there in the marsh was that mountain of brush. He figured he might could tunnel into the brushpile and make a cave where he might be safe from the bugs' attack. Where nobody, nor nothing could find him. And so, with sudden zeal, he dove at the brush, beating his way in through the branches and vines and long dead Christmas trees. Thorns and sharp sticks tore at his skin, but he learned to bash the brush back with his cast despite the pain, and after a while he had a decent little cave, and the bugs weren't so bad.

Only then, as soon as he stopped moving, every inch of his skin went up in a fire of itching-hurting Hell. He scratched himself until he bled all over, and he heard his Prayer Voice saying: *That's just right! That's just what you deserve, you Evil sinner.* But then he stopped that Voice again and hollered out loud, "No! Jesus is dead and gone and not a bit real! Just bullspit – No! Fuckin Bullshit! Just a

Bullshit lie adults made up to make you act right! Like Santy Claus or the dern – Damn! – Easter Bunny."

It was all just like that Visitin Preacher: all lies; every bit of it – sin and miracles, Heaven and Hell.

Charles Thomas felt empty and exhausted then. Hungry and thirsty as he'd ever been. His thirst made him dizzy and his hunger made him weak. There were locusts roosting in the brushpile. Their chanting drowned out every other sound. The earth smelled like ash from generations of fire on this spot. He scratched and scratched at his raw skin. And then he imagined everybody looking for him and getting all frantic that he'd disappeared or that something awful had happened to him. He imagined hiding out there for days until he died, and then one of them, his Mom or Furry, finding his swollen, bloody body and the whole island feeling so terrible that they'd forget they were ever mad at him.

Then he imagined a different ending: Red-Head-Steve, who worked for the town, would come and set fire to the brushpile without realizing Charles Thomas was in there until it was too late, and then everyone would know the story of his death and his final screams. Screams for Love and Forgiveness; that would make them all feel like Crapstains! All that suffering seemed deeply satisfying in a way, and finally he stopped crying. Everything felt distant then – except for the pain of his skin, his hunger, and his thirst – and then, again, a profound weakness and exhaustion smothered him whole and he slept like surrendering to death.

And that was when Charles Thomas had his vision: not a dream but a vision, for it was realer than anything he'd seen or felt all day. It was not like a dream, for he was still right where he was, alone in the brushpile. He could still hear the locusts all around him. And then there came a single locust. It landed on his broken arm and looked up at him. He could feel its weight adding to the pain in his arm. He realized it had the face of his Mom. She was his Mom, and she was accusing him of all he'd done. Then more and more locusts appeared, covering his broken body, all with faces of people that he knew – Furry, Rooster, Mr. Abe and Rodney, Dolores and her mum-mum, all the older kids, the Visitin Preacher and Remi – and all of them were crawling on his skin and accusing him. They got bigger and bigger and grew great gnashing fangs. Crabs with faces of all the people he knew on the island began swarming the earth and entering the brushpile to get at him. Then Dolores and her mum-mum transformed into a huge horrible beast. It had two heads and horns and thousands of eyes covering its body, all glaring at him with a hateful Judgment.

Then, with a paralyzing terror, he realized that this was The End, and immediately the sky turned black and he saw the Bay beside him turn to blood. A figure big as a mountain, dressed in a cloud and with legs like fiery pillars, came riding down upon him, mounted on a white horse with seven heads, like the heads of dragons all covered in horns. And when the figure drew close Charles Thomas saw that His skin was as black as the moonless, starless night. Charles Thomas cowered in his dream for he knew then how wrong he'd been: he hadn't found Jesus because he was searching for the wrong vision all along. But Jesus found him just the same. Jesus was real and His face was black as charcoal, and then this Black Christ opened his mouth and a fiery double-edged sword sprang forth. Charles Thomas knew at that moment that he was Damned for not having believed in the True Lord. And for all his sins – for exactly what he'd done to Mr. Abe and Rodney, and little Dolores alone in her sideyard. He stared into the face of the Black Christ. The bones showed through that dark skin, and the Black Christ had a beard that traced his jaw just like Mr. Abe's. And then that fiery sword came forward to Charles Thomas's throat, and in that instant he felt keenly that he'd lost his body and his body'd lost his head.

His eyes sprung open with a shock like he'd been electrocuted. A peal of thunder had ripped through the air so close and so powerful that it shook the marshy ground beneath him and made the great brushpile tremble around him like a bird in hand.

Both of Charles Thomas's legs and his good arm had gone numb with icy-fire[40] from the strange position in which he found himself. He realized with an all-consuming panic that he couldn't move his limbs, as if his body was no longer his own. Right above the island a flash of lightning tore the sky in two – its light could be seen in every direction for a long instant – and, before its light could even fade, another peal of thunder, still stronger than the last, shook the world like some great mountain crashing into the Earth.

Charles Thomas was gripped by a pure and wrenching terror unlike anything he'd ever felt. He smelled the scorched earth beneath him, and he knew in the depths of his soul that this was It and It was this. *Repent, Repent, Repent*, his Prayer Voice screeched. He tried to look out from his cave towards the sky, but it was as if the sun had

---

[40] 'Icy-fire': Jtown talk for pins and needles; tingling numbness.

turned black and his eyes were holes. Again the lightning flashed like an exploding star, and the thunder roared so that he could feel it in his nose and mouth. All he knew was fear, and he jammed his eyes shut and began to pray, saying, *Christ-a-mighty I'm sorry, I'm sorry for all my sins, for Rodney and Mr. Abe, for Dolores and Rooster and everything. Please, Black Jesus, let me be saved, let me be saved, and I promise I'll give ye anything! I'll give ye anything you ask*! He said it again and again and then the rain cut loose. Within seconds rain and hail were pelting the island with the roar of an invading army.

Through his terror and the rushing rain and the pounding hail, Charles Thomas half-heard the rumble of a motorcycle approach and come to a stop. A voice called his name, but Charles Thomas's head and limbs were still separate, and his tongue was frozen with horror. He wanted nothing so bad as to call out that he was there, but he couldn't for the life of him, and then the grumbling motor rose and the motorcycle left him behind.

Terror reigned then, for Charles Thomas knew that he had been left behind. He had lost his place amongst the chosen. He kept his eyes screwed shut, and in that darkness he saw his vision return: riding down from the Heavens astride that horse with its dragon heads, white robes flowing, legs afire and His skin just as black and big as the sky above. His sword came flaming from His mouth, and in His black hand was a book, bigger than the world. Charles Thomas felt a fear – greater than that of shame or loss or even death – that his name was not within those pages, and so he threw himself doubly into prayer, promising his life to that face of darkness. And then there came a strangely familiar voice that boomed from the Heavens and seemed to reverberate in every corner of the world. It said: "That Flood's a'comin. Every mountain and island'll be removed from its place. Speak only the Truth yer witnessed and let It be heard." These words repeated like a chant being scribed across his brain, and as the sound echoed on he realized why he knew that voice: it was the voice of his Father speaking straight to him. That thought came as an all-engulfing, all-mighty revelation, like some divine embrace. It meant that his Father was there still, seeing all and guiding Charles Thomas from a place on high.

As with any typical Chesapeake Bay summer thunderstorm the rain and the hail stopped as suddenly as they began. The thunder and lightning journeyed on to the east. It was a long time before Charles Thomas could move so much as his frozen eyelids, but at last, after what seemed like hours, he managed to pry them open.

The new light following the storm was gold and red, and after a while longer, he realized he was able to move his arms and legs again. At last he crawled out from his cave and stood like a newborn foal, all soaked and shivering. Sooty mud was plastered in his hair and in his ears. For the first time all day the locusts were silenced. Everything was silent but for the reverberation of his Father's words in his head.

Charles Thomas looked out across the landscape of his lifetime, and he saw it was all made new, re-colored by this new revelation. The storm had all but disappeared to the east. To the west the sun was huge and red, sinking into the Bay, which was just as red and glassy as a sea of blood. Opposite the sun – across the endless flatness of the marsh and water – was the full moon, red as well, and climbing in the sky. To Charles Thomas's newborn eyes that sun and that moon looked like two bloody holes piercing from one end of the Heavens to the other, just as prophesized.

Charles Thomas surveyed his town. The roofs were wet and the windows shone in the light of red and gold. All those buildings and all those lives within; they seemed so small and far-off now. His head spun wildly like a compass too near a magnet so that he couldn't be sure what was real and what was vision – what was Saved and what was

Damned. From this distance he saw how fragile, mortal and precarious this world of his truly was. He knew in the depths of his soul that the Second Flood was coming and his island stood no chance. Then Charles Thomas fully understood this Revelation: this Prophecy had been given to him to be their Salvation. He had been chosen; the Black Christ and his Father had come to him and him alone, and he alone knew Christ's true form and the way in which He came. Charles Thomas knew that he had promised his life and so was Saved, and he understood that he must go forth now and prophesize, to save the souls of everybody he knew. Through the light of this new responsibility he felt his own spirit leave his body and climb up into the sky to join his waiting Father. Everything was new now, the old order of things had passed away, and so the boy set off across the wilderness, returning without fear, nor shame, nor hate, to save this lost and dying world of his.

PETE FORTENBAUGH'S family roots go back to 1693 on the Delmarva Peninsula. The Chesapeake – its stories, culture and complicated human history – are in his blood. His earliest experiences were on boats, including six-months in his adolescence living aboard a catamaran with his family, a trip that whetted his appetite for traveling the world. He spent months trekking throughout Latin America, for two years lived in Spain where he taught English in public and private schools and earned a Masters in Teaching through the Universidad de Alcalá in 2018, then lived in Dakar, Senegal for eight months teaching English, which also helped to improve his French. Yet regardless of where he roams, his heart remains on the Eastern Shore.

Informed by the close friendships he made while living and working as a carpenter on isolated Tangier Island, Fortenbaugh's work explores with humor and compassion the characters and the often-complex relationships of the people of fictional Johnsontown, a racially mixed community of four hundred-plus souls.

A finalist for the prestigious Sophie Kerr Prize, the largest undergraduate literary award in the country, Fortenbaugh's work has been published in a variety of literary magazines and anthologies including: Niche Literary Magazine, Little Patuxent Review, and Washington Writers' Publishing House's 2021 anthology *This is What America Looks Like*. This is his first novella.

READ MORE of Pete Fortenbaugh's Johnsontown stories.

Excerpt of:

INHERITANCE *

"Ain't no way you can burry him under that house. Ain't no way. Yer Pap-Pap was crazier'an hellfire toward the end. Everbody knowed that."

"Welp, I promised it to him," the boy said.

The boy's Great-Uncle stood there scratching his old black lab's ear and shaking his head in the early morning sun.

"But he was crazier'an hell-fire," Roger said. "Gowan: ask any soul on the island. Nobody'd put no stock in nothing he said no more."

"Don't make no diffrence if he were crazy or not. I promised it to him, and that's all there is to it."

"You don't owe him a thing. He's got him a plot in Cambridge that Darlene and I paid for. They'll dig'er with a excavator and that's it. Funeral home'll organize it and dress him and everthing."

The boy stood there staring across the island, and the Bay beyond, his jaw set as straight as the horizon. "You know as well as me, he tolt ever soul that'd listen not to let them bury him off a this island. And to put him in the ground right under that house if there weretn't no other place that'd have him."

"But ye don't owe a dead man nothin. He's got him a place all set aside in Cambridge. Ain't like it makes a bit a diffrence to him now."

"Look Uncle Roger, I ain't got time for this. If ye don't wanta lend me that hand spade, I'll find one somewheres else."

"Awright, awright; I'll get'er for ye. But you know it don't make no diffrence." Roger limped off around the corner of his house, around back to the outhouse where he kept his gardening tools. His dog followed at his heel and he mumbled to it as he went, "Cain't talk common sense to them that ain't got none. Never heard nothin so crazy in all m'life."

The boy stayed in the front yard with his foot on the front step of his Great-Uncle's big house on West Water St. He fingered a cigarette and a lighter out of his coat pocket and lit it and looked up at the sky. It was November and the heavens were as clear and dry as a pane of glass. The sun had been up an hour; it was hollow-white: more cold than hot. He shivered and thought how miserable, muddy and wet it was going to be underneath the house. His Pap-Pap's brother came stumping back around the corner of his house holding a hand spade and a nice, new full-length shovel.

"Don't need the shovel. Pap-Pap's got one."

"Take it anyhow. I know what his tools is worth."

The boy took the shovel grudgingly, hating to admit what he knew to be true. "I'll bring'er by when I'm done," he said and started off towards the little house on Sun St.

"Me and Darlene'll be by within the hour to get him cleaned up and dressed."

The boy kept walking.

His Pap-Pap's house, where they both lived, had about the smallest plot of land on the whole island of Johnsontown. The entire walk along Sun St. the boy kept his eyes on the slumping little building. The house was two stories and had four windows facing the street. Chain-link fences were elbow-close on both sides. Over the years the phragmites had crept right up to the back step like a hungry herd of cats, and the whole building seemed to be leaning back onto its heels from where it had settled into the marsh. There was only a three-foot strip of front yard, and that was mostly occupied by two half-dead cedar bushes that scratched at the house when the wind blew west.

Their neighbor, a sun-dried, old black woman named Dot Johnson, was leaning on her chain-link fence, so close she could've reached out and touched the chimney of the old man's house.

"I'm sorry Noah," she said when the boy got close enough. "Mr. Ham was as good a man as I'm ever knowed, Christian or not."

"Nothin to be sorry about. He's getting the onliest thing he wanted."

"So you's gonna do it like he sayed?"

"It's the onliest thing I can do."

Full story published in the Winter 2021 issue of Little Patuxent Review.

Acknowledgements

I need to thank so many people. My Mom and Dad, brother Will, Aunt Barb, Meredith and all of my family for being so full of love and support. Nancy Robson for working so hard on this book and on all of my writing for so many years, and the Robson family, especially Matt for his reading and solid advice. My art contributors: Tilly Castelli for her illustrations, Ken Castelli for his map, Zack Schmitt for his cover design, and Bennett Price for his author photo. Vicco and the von Voss family for their many years of friendship, employment and nurturing. Bob Mooney for teaching me how to write, along with James Allen Hall, the Sophie Kerr Committee, and all of the teachers who have inspired me over the years. The Hawkridge family for being great readers and even better friends. August Thompson for his readership and insights. My friends on Tangier: Whid Eskridge, Jim and Leigh Shores, Fuzz, Katie and Jack Mariano, Cameron Evans, Carol Pruitt-Moore and Lonnie Moore, along with everybody else who welcomed me and employed me on the island. And, most important, to all of my beloved friends across the country and all around the world with whom I've shared so much.

Made in the USA
Middletown, DE
09 October 2021